D1413098

Praise for *Cotton Candy Wishes*

"Oh, the sweet and sour of seventh grade. Taylor Hunt experiences it all in Kristina Springer's deliciously realistic *Cotton Candy Wishes*."
—Cindy Callaghan, Just Add Magic series, Lost In series, and *Sydney Mackenzie Knocks 'Em Dead*

"*Cotton Candy Wishes* illustrates that true friends—and not popularity—are the sweetest dessert of all."
—Gail Nall, author of *Out of Tune* and *Break the Ice*

"Tweens will love this sweet story about following your heart even when it's not exactly easy."
—Lisa Schroeder, author of *It's Raining Cupcakes* and *See You on a Starry Night*

"Springer deftly captures the highs and lows of junior high, taking the reader through the full range of emotions."
—Jo Whittmore, author of the Confidentially Yours series

CURL UP WITH ALL OF THE SWIRL NOVELS!

Pumpkin Spice Secrets by Hillary Homzie
Peppermint Cocoa Crushes by Laney Nielson
Cinnamon Bun Besties by Stacia Deutsh
Salted Caramel Dreams by Jackie Nastri Bardenwerper
Apple Pie Promises by Hillary Homzie
Cotton Candy Wishes by Kristina Springer

COTTON CANDY WISHES

Kristina Springer

Sky Pony Press
New York

To Teegan, Maya, London, and Gavin—
may you always have friends who really matter.

Chapter One
PARTY TIME!

"Taylor, it's fine!" Mom calls out to me without looking up. She's concentrating hard on the giant cotton candy machine in front of her, spinning a cotton candy cone around and around in the web of sticky pink floss, trying to load the perfect amount onto it. It's the tenth practice cotton candy she's made today.

The sweet smell in the air makes my mouth water, but I'm not having any cotton candy until the party starts. I tap my chin with my index finger and survey the configuration of large bowls in front of me. I know Mom thinks I'm obsessing over the appetizer buffet table, but it still doesn't look right to me. There are too many tortilla-based chips clustered together. We need a better candy-to-chip ratio for optimal appeal. Like, it should go Nacho Cheese Doritos, M&Ms, potato chips, gummy worms, Cheetos. Not Nacho Cheese, Cool Ranch, Jumpin' Jack, and Extreme Chili flavored Doritos all right next to each other. It's Dorito overkill.

I can feel the butterflies fluttering in my stomach as I set to rearranging the bowls of food. Absolutely everyone is going to be here today, and it has to be just right. I'm practically jumping out of my skin envisioning the stream of kids who will be filing into my backyard any second now. It's my first boy-girl party, and I've invited the entire seventh grade. All seventy-five kids. This is huge.

I set back down the M&Ms and notice the giant glass dish of pink gumballs is missing. Mom ordered them online for me to specifically match the cotton-candy theme of my birthday party. I glance around the yard, wondering where I might have left them.

Mom and I have been working on my big twelfth-birthday bash for weeks. We'd thought it would have to be in our basement; but the late fall weather is cooperating and it is only sixty-five degrees out so we moved it into the backyard. Dad even said we could have a bonfire when the sun begins to set. I'm so excited! This is already going to be the best party ever, but an added bonfire with the necessary s'mores definitely bumps it up a notch.

We've strung cotton candy lights all along the fence, which were surprisingly simple to make thanks to Pinterest. We just took regular white twinkle lights, lots of cotton, and pink spray paint and rolled loads of pieces of white paper to make the cones. After a little time and effort with Mom's glue gun, we were done. And the result was fantastic. I want to keep and hang them all up in my room after the party. Then I'll always remember this night.

"Aha!" I yell, spotting my ten-year-old sister, Sophie, sitting in the small wood house at the top of our playset. She has the bowl of gumballs in her lap. "Sophie! That's for guests!"

Sophie blows a giant bubble at me. After it pops, she says, "What? I'm a guest."

I narrow my eyes at her and place my hands on my hips. "You don't count."

Sophie shoots me a wounded look and sticks another gumball in her mouth.

I ramble up the skinny ladder, snatch the bowl

away from her, and then return it to the buffet table with the rest of the food.

My best friend Nora is sitting at one of the long, pink tablecloth–covered tables, her arms folded across her stomach. "I'm not feeling that great," she says.

I cross the yard and reach her quickly. "What's wrong?"

Nora has a half-eaten cotton candy in each hand. "Your mom keeps making me eat her test cotton candy cones."

I give Nora a sympathetic look. Nora is so polite. She's probably afraid to tell Mom she's not hungry or that she's had enough. And Nora's mom keeps their whole family on an all-organic, sugar-free diet so all this candy is probably really taking a toll on her. "Aw, Nora, you don't have to eat anymore. I'll tell her to stop passing them to you."

Nora returns a weak smile. "It's okay."

"Here, let me get rid of those." I hold out my hands and Nora drops the cotton candies into them. I walk over to one of the large trash cans and dump them in and then zip up my fuzzy pink North Face fleece coat. I wore it special today with my favorite jeans and pink converse shoes to coordinate with the decor.

Mom even found me the cutest, tiny cotton candy earrings. I reach up and touch one of them with my index finger.

I fell in love with cotton candy at Lucas Sanchez's eighth birthday party. He had invited Mr. Miller's entire homeroom class of thirty kids and everyone had so much fun. It was at one of those trampoline places and we jumped and did flips and danced to the music pumping through the giant warehouse. Back then, everyone got along and there were no cliques or groups. No one was popular or unpopular. I remember feeling so happy at that party. And when we were all sweaty and tired from jumping, Lucas's mom gave us each a massive cone of cotton candy. It tasted so good. Each time I have cotton candy now, I remember that day and that feeling. Maybe, hopefully, people will have cotton candy at my party and remember an equally awesome time with friends.

Dad's outside now and has taken over cotton-candy-making duties while Mom wipes at her arms. She somehow has gotten the pink sugary fluff all over herself.

"Sophie, you want one?" Dad calls. He's smiling as he swirls the cone around like he's having the best time.

Sophie pops another bubble and ignores him.

We'd made dozens and dozens of cotton-candy topped cupcakes, loads of pink salted cotton candy popcorn, and we have cotton candy hot chocolate in jars all ready to go. Sophie and I tested these out last week and watching the cotton candy disappear as you add the hot water to it is so cool. I spent most of last weekend making bag after bag of cotton candy slime putty for kids to take home as their goody bag gift. For centerpieces, we made pink cotton candy bouquets that we set in old-fashioned soda bottles and spray-painted white. Everything looks amazing.

This is the hardest I've ever worked on any party. I've only ever had small parties with just a few friends so inviting my entire grade like this is a pretty big deal for me. This is the party that is going to change everything. This is how I'm going to make loads more friends, so the details are critical. I may even move into the popular crowd after today. It's not that I don't have any friends; I do. Nora, Anusha, Julie, and I are always together at school. I just don't have a ton of them. I've always dreamed of being the center of a huge, cool group of kids. Of not having to worry about who I'll eat lunch with if my friends are out sick, or who

I'll partner up with in gym since none of my friends are in that class with me. On that day, two weeks ago, when I personally passed out all of the party invitations that I'd made myself, and people smiled and thanked me, I knew I was doing the right thing.

"Hey, Tay," Sophie calls out.

I finish restacking the pink plastic cups next to the punch bowl and look up. "Yeah?" I fan my face. I'm actually starting to sweat with all of this running around even though the air is cool.

"Didn't you say your party started at five?"

"Yeah," I say again.

"It's 5:45," she says matter-of-factly.

"No, it's not." I pull my phone out of my pocket and tap the home button to turn it on. Sophie is right. It is 5:45 p.m. I bite my bottom lip.

"Maybe no one wants to be first at a party," I say after a few moments have passed. I notice my mouth feels dry and my hand holding the phone is starting to tremble. I shove my phone back into my pocket and clasp my shaky hand with my other one.

"Hey, I was the first," Nora says.

I tilt my head toward Nora. "But you're my best friend," I tell her. I wrack my brain for other possibilities. "Maybe their parents are looking for parking."

"That's probably it," Nora agrees, her head bobbing up and down.

I know that we both know there is plenty of parking on the street in front of my house.

I pull one of the folded invitations out of my pocket and reread it. It's in the shape of a giant cotton candy and my big swoopy writing fills out every line. I definitely wrote five o'clock on it.

"Did you get any RSVPs?" Nora asks.

I look down toward the ground and kick at the heel of my right foot with my left toe. "No. I didn't ask for them. I thought it would seem lame if I did."

"Oh," Nora says.

We're both quiet. A heavy weight forms in the pit of my stomach. I stumble to the closest chair at the opposite end of the table from Nora and plop down before I fall down. A trickle of sweat slides down my back.

I look over at Mom. Her and Dad pass worried looks back and forth and then give me sympathetic smiles. That's when I realize no one is coming to my party.

"Here, sweetie, have a cotton candy," Mom says,

rushing toward me and shoving a massive ball of the pink stuff into my hand.

I accept the cone and turn away from my family and Nora. I squeeze my eyes shut tight, trying hard not to cry. But it doesn't work. Big tears roll down my face. I open my eyes and watch as they plop into my cotton candy, making tiny fizzing holes as they dissolve the sugar.

"Jim," Mom hisses from behind me. "Bring over the cupcakes. Light the candles. Sophie, get over here."

I blink hard and take deep breaths, trying to calm down. I reach up one hand and wipe at my cheeks. *It's going to be okay*, I tell myself. *It's going to be okay.*

I fix a smile on my face and slide back around in my seat. Dad, Mom, Sophie, and Nora are standing behind a massive platter of cupcakes, twelve of them lit for me. They carefully set them down on the table in front of me and sing Happy Birthday. Mom sings loud, as though she was singing in a football stadium. Maybe she thinks this will help me forget that no one else is here.

When they finish singing, Mom says, "Make a wish, Taylor."

I wish I was popular, I think and blow out the candles.

Chapter Two
WORST. DAY. EVER.

The rest of the weekend dragged by. Not that I was super overjoyed to get to school this morning, though. I felt like I'd gone through every emotion there was in the last day and a half. I went from excitement to devastation to denial. Then I felt really, really sorry for myself. And now I'm just mad. Mad at myself for thinking I could have a big fancy party and everyone would be happy to come and want to be my friend and mad at my entire class for not showing up.

I've been fairly quiet all morning, not that any- one has noticed. I sat alone in the cafeteria before first bell, just staring at my phone like I was read- ing something super interesting when I was really eavesdropping on the conversations the kids around me were having. A group of girls chatted about something hilarious that happened at their dance competition over the weekend and some boys talked about an all-night online Fortnite party they'd had. Part of me wished someone would notice me and include me in their conversation or ask me how my birthday was. And part of me was glad to just be left alone. My friend Julie tried to talk to me a little in science class, but I told her I had a headache. I couldn't believe she hadn't even asked me about my birthday party or offered an excuse for her absence. When the bell for lunch rang, I shuffled slowly to the cafeteria and got in the hot lunch line.

Nora joins me and chats away happily. "Are you guys reading *The Outsiders* in English class too? It's so old, like, I think it was written in the sixties? Why can't we read a current book? Do you guys get to watch the movie? We're going to once we're done reading. We have to get a permission slip signed by our parents. Who names their kids Ponyboy and Sodapop anyway?"

I look up at her but don't even try to reply to any of the questions that she's firing off. Doesn't she know

I am still hurting from my humiliation on Saturday? I don't want to talk about English class or any book right now.

I pick up a tray holding a chicken patty sandwich, mixed vegetables, and mashed potatoes off the counter and slide my school ID to the cashier. I wait for Nora while she pays for her lunch and we walk to our usual lunch table where Anusha and Julie are already sitting. They both look up and smile when we sit down.

"Hey!" Nora says.

The girls both say hi.

I push the plastic spoon out of its cellophane wrapper and stab at my mashed potatoes.

"How was your birthday party, Taylor?" Anusha asks.

I raise my eyes and look at her to see if she's kidding. She bats her big brown eyes at me innocently. Out of the corner of my eye, I see Nora give the girls a head shake. They must not have heard yet.

"It's okay, Nora," I say. "I'll tell them. My party sucked. Nobody showed up. Except for Nora. It was a party of me, Nora, my mom, my dad, and Sophie."

Julie brings one hand to her mouth in surprise. "Oh, no," she whispers.

Anusha's eyes go wide. "I'm so sorry, Taylor. You remember I had my cousin's first birthday party, right? I told you right after I got your invitation and talked to my mom. She wouldn't let me out of it."

I nod slowly. I sort of do remember that conversation. But I hadn't thought a one-year-old would have a party in the evening so I figured she still would have been able to make my mine.

"And I had ice skating," Julie interjects. "You know how my mom is."

I sigh. That was true too. We all know Mrs. Wu never lets Julie miss ice time. Julie has to practice two hours before school, two hours after school, plus all day Saturdays. It's pretty intense.

"Did you get my text?" Anusha asks.

I nod. I do have several unopen texts sitting in my phone right now. I was too angry to open them over the weekend. I rub my forehead with my right hand. Julie and Anusha did have valid excuses but it doesn't make the whole thing sting any less. "I know, guys. I'm not mad at you. I'm mad at them."

I let my gaze roam around the cafeteria at the tables bursting with kids. Some tables have so many kids packed tightly around them that it looks like they can't even move their arms to eat. There are the sporty kids and the honors kids. The popular kids and the band kids. They joke and laugh and look like they're having the best lunches ever. And here I sit with my only three friends in the world. If they all got strep throat on the same day, I'd be eating lunch by myself. None of the other kids in my grade seemed to care that they missed my party. None of them cared enough to even wish me a belated happy birthday. It's pretty depressing.

I tuck a piece of my long, blonde hair behind my ear. "I thought I could change things by inviting everyone to a great party. But I bet they didn't even give my invitation a second thought. I worked so hard on the party, too."

The three girls exchange sad looks.

"Aw, Taylor, don't let it get you down," Anusha says.

"Yeah, it really was a nice party," Nora says. "You could be a party planner or something. Everything looked so cool."

I give Nora a small smile. It really did.

"What can we do to make it up to you, Taylor?" Julie asks.

"Yeah, we feel really bad," Anusha chimes in.

I shrug. "It's fine. You don't have to do anything." Short of inventing a time machine and then making everyone show up, nothing is going to change what happened.

"Maybe we can have a sleepover at my house this weekend?" Anusha asks. "We can play D&D and watch movies."

I almost smile. She knows I love D&D. My dad got me into the role-playing game years ago.

Anusha's smooth, long black ponytail swings behind her as she whips her head to the side to look at Julie. "Would your mom let you come?"

"Um . . . well," Julie stammers. She clears her throat.

"Really, don't worry about it," I snap. I know I sound a bit harsh, but I'm not in the mood to hear any other excuses for why my friends can't be there for me. Besides, a sleepover at *Anusha's* house isn't going to make me feel any better about no one coming to *my* party.

An uproar of laughter from a nearby table catches my attention. Five girls, all sporting fashionable outfits and trendy makeup, crowd around one phone. These are the most popular girls in our grade. I used to be friends with one of the girls, Allison, back in elementary school. But when we got to junior high, the class clearly divvied up and she went with the popular group and I fell into . . . whatever you'd call me and my tiny group of friends. Ever since, Allison has acted like she doesn't have a clue who I am, let alone that we were ever even friends. The girls giggle again and a couple of them hop around and hug the one holding the phone. Something exciting must be happening to her.

I keep watching the popular girls and can't help thinking that none of them would have missed their best friend's birthday party. I try to picture myself as the girl in the middle of the group with all of her friends gathered around her, paying her so much attention. It's a happy thought. But then I remember that I'm not her, I'm me.

"Let me just ask my mom, Taylor," Julie says. "I'm sure I can work something out."

I give Julie a weak smile, feeling bad for having snapped at her. I'm sure she really does mean well.

I push my lunch tray away from me, unable to eat. "You know what, guys? I'm not feeling all that great. I'll be back in a few minutes."

"Want me to come with you?" Nora asks, concern in her eyes.

"Nah," I reply. "I think I'm going to just splash some cold water on my face." I stand, push in my chair, and head for the girls' bathroom.

Once I'm safely tucked into the furthest stall inside the bathroom, near the wall, I perch on the toilet seat and pull my legs up, wrapping my arms around my knees. I just need a few minutes alone to collect my thoughts, and then I'll be ready to face the rest of this day.

Only a few minutes have gone by when I hear a couple of girls talking to each other in front of the mirrors. They're talking loudly and don't seem to have noticed that they are not alone in the bathroom. I hold still, not wanting to draw any attention to myself.

"Did you go to that nerdy math girl's party?" one of the girls asks.

A chill shoots straight through me. They couldn't possibly be talking about me, could they?

"That princess pony one or whatever?" the other girl asks.

The first girl laughs. "I think it was cotton candy, actually. Same level of lame, though."

"Oh, gawd, no," the second girl says. "I threw that invitation out right after she gave it to me."

"Yeah, I was never going to go either. I felt bad when she gave it to me, though. She was handing them out to everyone. Poor, clueless thing."

"Desperate."

"Totally."

I put my hands over my ears and push hard. I can't hear any more of this. My heart is pounding, and tears are rolling down my face. These mean, horrible girls!

I sit like this, rocking and crying softly to myself, until I hear the bell ring indicating the end of the lunch hour. I peek out from the stall and see that I'm alone in the bathroom. I let myself out, splash water on my face, and then head out of the bathroom into the sea of students headed for sixth period.

Worst. Day. Ever. After that terrible scene in the girls' bathroom during lunch, I couldn't get it out of my mind that everyone else must be thinking and saying awful things about me, too. Every time I saw two kids with their heads together, talking and laughing, which is practically every five minutes in junior high, I was positive they were talking about me and my party. I couldn't stop thinking that everyone thought I was weird and that my party was a joke. The school day couldn't end fast enough. As I climbed down the bus steps that afternoon, I couldn't wait to get to my room, shut the door, and try to forget about the awfulness of today. As if Saturday hadn't already been bad enough.

I walk in through our front door, drop my bag on the ground, and shrug off my coat. I had decided on the ride home that I wouldn't let my parents know what had happened at school. I know my mom, and I know she'd instantly burst into tears, too, if she knew what I'd overheard today. And then she'd want names and phone number of parents so she could yell at someone.

I'm mentally going through my homework assignments for the evening, trying to organize in order of importance. My plan is to get through my homework quickly, have dinner, and go to bed early. I realize that I have something to do in almost all of my classes, and I sigh inwardly. Seventh grade is so much harder than sixth grade. The teachers really pile on the work.

I head for my room but hear my parents talking in the kitchen. *This is strange*, I think, *why is Dad home so early?* I take a few steps closer and lean in to hear.

"I can't believe this is really happening, Jim," Mom says. She sounds miserable. "The girls are several months into the school year. How can we just yank them out like this?"

Yank us out of school? I think. *No way.* I move even closer, making sure I'm sufficiently hidden behind the wall. If my parents knew I was eavesdropping, they'd be furious.

"I know, hon, I know," Dad says. He sighs loudly. "I'm not happy about any of this either. It's completely out of my hands."

"I know it is," Mom replies. "It's not your fault that they're transferring you. I just wish there was some way they could figure out something else for you to do here. How do they expect you to just pick up your whole life and go like this? We have a family."

"Believe me, I've wracked my brain trying to come up with an alternative solution. They're eliminating my position here, so I can either move to another branch or look for a new job. I could always turn down the transfer, but it could take months for me to find something."

"And we're a single-income family," Mom adds. "We can't go without a paycheck."

"Our hands are tied," Dad concludes, his voice laced with sadness.

"But two hours south?" Mom says, sounding distraught again. "What's in central Illinois anyway? Isn't it all corn fields? We're so close to the city now. We'll never get back up to Chicago if we move so far away."

"Sure we will," Dad says, trying to sound positive. "It just won't be as often."

"The girls will be devastated," she continues. "We're going to rip them away from everything they know . . . all of their friends."

All of my friends, I think. *Ha!*

"I know," Dad replies. "That's the worst part. But they're kids. They'll adjust. They might even do better in a small town."

I strain to hear but Mom isn't saying anything.

Finally, Dad says, "I've already put a deposit on a house to rent until we sell this house and find something we want to buy out there. We can move in in two weeks."

"Two weeks?" Mom says, sounding a little frantic now. "There's so much to do. We'll have to pack up the whole house, turn off services, list this house for sale, enroll the girls in the new school . . ."

"We'll do it together. It'll all get done," Dad assures her.

I quietly move away from my hiding spot, tiptoe up the stairs to my room, and shut my bedroom door safely behind me. I let a huge smile slowly spread across my face. I know Mom and Dad are upset, but I don't think this will be as bad as they're thinking. I think just the opposite. I'm sorta thrilled that we're moving. Aside from Nora, Anusha, and Julie, I don't have any friends here anyway. A change of scenery might be just what I need.

Chapter Three
CHANGE IS COMING

Whap. . . . Whap.

Sophie is lying on her back on my bed with her feet up the wall, whipping a small neon rainbow-colored bouncy ball at the ceiling and then catching it.

I look up from the box that I just dumped the contents from my top desk drawer into and glare at the top of her head. "Could you stop that? You're going to leave marks."

"So? It won't be your room anymore soon anyway. Why do you care?"

"Mom and Dad will care if they have to repaint the ceiling," I return. I take the cap off my black sharpie and label the side of the box, *desk stuff*. "Besides, shouldn't you be packing up your own bedroom?"

Sophie lives across the hall in a room we long ago nicknamed The Pit. It's truly disgusting. I can't even remember what color the carpet is in there since I haven't seen it in years. Sophie lives among mountains of clothes, toys, papers, and random junk. I've even seen old lollipop sticks and empty string cheese wrappers strewn around in there. She throws away nothing. Mom gave up on cleaning her room years ago because Sophie just destroys it again in less than twenty-four hours. We all avoid going in there if we can, which I think Sophie secretly loves and is the reason behind her filthy hoarder ways. She won't even keep her bed clear. She just pushes all the junk out of the way to make a circle in the middle to sleep in and she calls it her nest. Like she's a bird. But no bird would ever go into that room.

"Nah," she says and resumes throwing the ball against the ceiling. "I'm not packing."

I stop what I'm doing and look at my sister. "What do you mean, you're not packing? You have to. Mom and Dad aren't going to step foot in your room. Unless it's just to shovel all that junk into garbage bags."

"They don't need to. I'm not moving." She tosses the ball at the ceiling once, twice, three more times.

"Of course, you are," I say. "We all are."

"Not me." *Whap . . . whap.*

"What, are you going to live here alone? I don't think Mom and Dad will go for that."

"Nope. I'm going to talk Grandma into moving in with me. She can bring a couple of her friends along too. It'll all be very *Golden Girls* except I'll be the young, fun version of Sophia, bringing all the mischief and drama."

Mom watches reruns of the *Golden Girls* on the weekends while she's cleaning the house. She says she was obsessed with watching them when she was our age and it's like revisiting old friends when she watches the reruns now. The image of what Sophie's suggesting fills my mind, and I start to giggle.

Just then, Mom throws open my bedroom door and I practically jump right out of my skin.

"What on earth is that horribly annoying, repetitive thumping I'm hearing?" she demands.

Sophie clutches the just caught ball in her hand and slowly moves into a sitting position.

I shoot her an I-told-you-so look from behind Mom's back.

"Sorry," she mumbles.

Mom surveys the already sealed boxes in stacks around my bedroom. "Looking good, Tay."

I smile. "Thanks."

Mom turns her attention to Sophie. "What about you, Soph? Have you filled all the boxes that I gave you already?"

Sophie lowers her eyes. "Not exactly." She crosses her arms over her chest.

"Shouldn't you be in your room working, then? You know we're short on time."

Sophie shakes her head no and sets her jaw in defiance.

Mom sighs and rubs her forehead. She looks tired. She's been packing up the kitchen all day. She slides onto my bed next to Sophie. "What's the problem, Sophie-bear?"

Sophie's chin wiggles, and she looks like she's going to cry. "It's not fair. I don't want to move. Why does Dad have to be transferred?"

Mom pats the bed for me to join them, and I take a seat. She gives me a sad smile. "I know this is tough on you girls. Change is always hard. But it's something we have to do as a family. We're all in this together. And you never know, you might even like where we're moving to. It could have the greatest school ever where you'll find your very best friend in the world."

"Not me," Sophie says. "I'm going to hate it like crazy. I don't want a new best friend. I want to keep my regular old friends here."

I give Sophie a sympathetic look. I can kind of see what she's saying. I'm going to miss Nora, Anusha, and Julie, too.

"I'm going to be so lonely," Sophie continues. "When am I ever going to see my friends again?"

Mom looks like she's thinking. "Well, there's always video chat and email. And maybe we can take a weekend trip every so often and come back this way," she suggests.

Sophie shakes her head firmly. "It won't happen. We'll go away and never come back. And everyone will forget all about me."

"Oh, Soph. You'll make new friends, you'll see," Mom says.

Sophie still looks miserable. I don't think she

believes that for a second. It's too bad she doesn't look at this move as an opportunity like I do. Mom is right; Sophie will make tons of friends as soon as she gets there. Sophie and I are so different. She's super popular, and everyone likes her. And I only have a handful of friends. She's sporty, and I hate anything athletic. She's outgoing and funny, and I usually try to blend in with the background.

A blast of nervousness hits me. What if I get to this new school and I'm just as unpopular as I am now? At least at my current school I have a few friends. What if everyone hates me at the new school? I never considered that things could get worse. I guess all I can do is hope that my birthday wish comes true, and I'll be popular at the new school.

I glance at Mom and she's leaned over, hugging Sophie. "Just give it a chance, Soph."

And an idea comes to me. What if I don't just sit around, waiting for wishes to come true? What if there is something I can do to make my wish actually happen?

A wave of excitement washes over me as a plan begins to lay out in my mind. I have to talk to my friends.

"I'll tell you what," Mom starts, "let's go bake a batch of brownies. That always cheers you up."

Sophie raises her head and a look of slight interest crosses her face. "But you already packed up the kitchen,"

Mom shrugs. "That's okay. I can dig out a bowl and a pan, I'm sure. Sound good?"

Sophie gives her a small smile and nods.

It was the right thing to say. Sophie is a total chocoholic and Mom knows it.

"Coming, Taylor?" Mom asks, stretching as she climbs off the bed.

I'm itching to run my idea past my friends. And make a list. I definitely need a list. "Nah, you guys go ahead. I'll help you eat them, though," I add.

"Okay, it's you and me, Soph."

As soon as Mom and Sophie leave my room, I shut the door behind them, grab my phone, and jump back onto my bed.

I start a group text to my friends. They had asked what they could do to cheer me up and I think I have just the thing. *You guys*, I write. *I need your help.*

I stare at the screen as their replies roll in.

Sure, Anusha sent.

Julie sends a thumbs-up emoji.

What's up? Nora asks.

I smile to myself as I type, *I need your help making me popular.*

Chapter Four
THE PLAN

I pull down the passenger seat rearview mirror and look at my friends. Julie, Nora, and Anusha all grin at me from the backseat. Mom is dropping us off at the mall to shop while she shops next door at Target. It's our first time getting to walk the mall alone, and we're all super excited.

Project Make Taylor Popular is under way.

When I first texted my friends about my idea last night, they were a bit skeptical. Okay, they thought I was crazy. Julie said she didn't know the first thing about being popular. Nora said I should just be myself. Which was a nice sentiment but completely unrealistic. I've already been myself for twelve years. I want to try something else. And Anusha offered to bring me a stack of her older sister's *Seventeen* magazine back issues for research. They're in our car trunk right now. Though they were initially cynical, everyone said they would help me and we brainstormed some ideas. We're going to compare more notes today.

Mom pulls up outside one of the mall entrances, near the Von Maur. "Okay, girls," she says, "I expect you to be on your best behavior. I'm only going to be two minutes away. Taylor, you have your phone, right?"

"Yes, Mom."

"Call me if there are any problems at all. I'll be back in about an hour or so, and I'll come find you girls."

"Great. Bye, Mom." I push open the passenger door and jump out. My friends file out the backseat.

"Bye, Mrs. Hunt," they each say.

Soon as we meet on the sidewalk, the four of us link arms and bounce as we rush into the mall.

"Freedom!" Nora cries out.

"Yes!" Anusha says.

We push into the mall, and I turn around and wave to my mom before she drives off. Then I turn back to my friends and say, "Okay, where first?"

"Food court?" Julie suggests.

"Yes, I want a frappe," Anusha says.

I consider this. A frappe isn't a bad way to start our mall trip. And it gives us time to sit and compare notes before tackling my list. "Let's do it," I say.

Anusha, Julie, and I grab our drinks from the pick-up counter at Mean Beans and find seats at a nearby table in the food court.

Julie takes a long sip of her vanilla frappe. She closes her eyes and grins. "Yum, this is so good."

I take a sip from mine and nod in agreement.

"Ooh, what did you get, Taylor?" Nora asks me when she rejoins us. She went to Jamba Juice for a green smoothie instead. "It looks cool."

"It's a cotton candy frappe," I reply, holding the bright pink concoction up in the air for her to get a better look. "It's on their secret menu. My mom got me one when we were here shopping for my party."

Nobody speaks as we recall my birthday disaster, a.k.a. the worst day of my life. But, I remind myself, that was in the past and I'm going to focus only on the future. A brighter, more popular future at my new school, where I'll never be ditched for my birthday again.

I take a long sip of the sweet vanilla-and-raspberry-syrup blend. It's delicious.

"Okay," I say, breaking the awkward silence. I pull a piece of paper out of my pocket and smooth it out on the table. "Let's get organized."

Julie looks relieved. I know she felt really bad about not coming to my birthday party and didn't want to rehash it again.

Anusha looks equally grateful for the change in subject.

Both girls probably had to do a lot of persuading with their parents to even be here today, and I appreciate the efforts they've made.

"Is that your list?" Anusha asks.

I nod. I worked on it for over an hour last night after we'd stopped texting. It contained all of my ideas for what I could do to be popular in the new school. The first item on my list was to get cute, super-fashionable clothes. I've scraped together all of the money I've saved from past birthdays and Christmases to use. Plus, Mom gave me an extra fifty dollars to spend on anything I want.

Nora gives the list a glance. "I think we should start with your look. We don't know much about where you're moving to, but with the Internet, I'm guessing the fashions are all pretty much the same. Personally, I've never kept up with what's fashionable. But I spent some time on the H&M and Forever 21 websites last night to see what's in style. Like glitter boots and fringe."

"Fringe? Like, cowgirl kind of fringe?" I ask. I had no idea fringe was in. It actually sounds kind of awful. I'm hoping it's not really a thing.

Nora thinks about this. "I'm not really sure. I guess we'll have to see it. I'm sure it's much trendier than it sounds. And lavender. We have to find you something in lavender. It's the 'it' color right now." She makes air quotation marks with her first two fingers on each hand.

I nod. I can do lavender. I pull a pen out of my purse and scribble, *Fringe?* And add *Lavender* to my list.

"How will you do your hair? I think you should try wearing your hair in a bun," Julie says. "Buns are so pretty, and I've noticed a lot of the popular girls in our grade wear them."

I write, *Bun?* on the paper.

"My mom wants me to get a haircut later today, but I'll make sure it stays long enough for a bun."

"Or even just a partial bun?" Julie says. "You know, where you just do your bangs pulled back into a bun?" She pulls a squared section of her long dark hair away from her forehead and twists it up on her head. "Like this."

"That looks great," Nora says. "You should wear your hair like that, Julie."

Julie shrugs and lets her hair fall back around her shoulders.

"My sister thinks she's hot stuff and she wears leggings all the time," Anusha says. "We should probably get you some of those."

I look down at my jean-clad legs. I usually feel cold in leggings. And I've always been partial to pants with pockets. But I can give leggings a try. I add *leggings* to the paper.

"Did you ask your sister for any other advice for me?" I ask Anusha.

She nods. "Yeah. She said trendy clothes are nice but it's all in the attitude. You have to walk around acting like you're super cool and everyone else will believe it too."

"So, confidence," Julie says. "That's just like in skating. I can perfect my jumps, spins, and combinations, but if my head is a mess before a competition, like, if I'm saying negative stuff to myself like I'll never land that double, then I'm totally thrown off. There's a lot of mental to competitions."

I bite my lower lip and nod. "That totally makes sense."

"Even if you don't feel confident," Nora says to me, "you can fake it. 'Fake it 'til you make it' is what my Dad always says. He's in sales, you know. He says even if you don't know something, you never let the client know that. Because then they'll lose confidence in you. You have to pretend like you know exactly what to do and then go figure it out when they're not around."

I pull my list toward me and write, *CONFIDENCE* in all caps and then add the line, *Fake it 'til you make it.* There.

I look up at my friends and smile. I'm so touched that they've not only taken my plan seriously, but they've even done some research and brought me such great ideas.

Anusha drains her frappe cup, making a slurping sound. "Ready to shop?" she asks.

"Let go," I say.

We hit Forever 21 first, where I find an adorable mini corduroy overall dress. I'm usually not big into dresses but it was seriously cute. And Nora was happy when she found me a long-sleeve lavender tee to go under it. We didn't find anything with fringe on it, but Anusha picked out a cool graphic tee for me that said FEMINIST across the front. We found tons of clearance leggings at H&M and a boyfriend cardigan at Hollister. And I had just enough left over for a Pink slouchy crew from Victoria Secret.

"Are you out of money yet?" Nora asks me as we walk through the mall.

"Just about. All I have left is three dollars in change and a twenty-dollar gift card for Claire's."

"I love Claire's," Julie says.

"Me too," I tell her.

We walk into the store and take in all the fun, brightly colored rows of jewelry. There is so much to look at. We spin the carousels of earrings and rings and I glance at the wall of phone cases.

"The girl on last month's cover of *Seventeen* was wearing one of these," Anusha says, holding a choker of tiny gold stars out to me.

I take it and run one finger along the stars. "It's

super cool. What do you think?" I ask, turning to Nora and Julie. I hold the choker up to my neck.

The girls bob their heads up and down.

"Get it," Nora says.

My phone buzzes with a text. I pull it out of my pocket and read the message. "It's my mom. She wants us to meet her at the haircut place near Bath and Bodyworks." I type out, *be right there* and hit send. "I better hurry up and buy this," I tell my friends.

I take the choker and head for the cashier. As I'm checking out, I notice a set of four corded friendship bracelets near the register, a different crystal hanging from each. I mentally add up the total of the choker and the bracelets, including tax. I love numbers and have always been able to do math quickly in my head. I decide that I have just enough for the entire purchase and I'm going to give one bracelet to each of the girls to remember me by and as a thank-you for helping me. I'll admit, I've been a bit standoffish with the group since my party disaster, but they've made up for it today. I know I'll miss these girls after I move; but I can't help feeling super excited about the possibilities that lie ahead. If I do this right, there's a real chance I can make a ton of new friends and never spend another birthday alone.

Chapter Five
THE FIRST DAY

Deep breath in and hold it for three, two, one, and let it out. Again. Deep breath in and let it out. I can do this. Washington Junior High School isn't going to know what hit it.

I open my eyes and look into the large oval mirror hanging over my dresser. My bangs are pulled up away from my face and twisted into a small bun like Julie had suggested, with the rest of my hair hanging down my back; and it really is pretty cute. After countless hours spent watching makeup tutorials on YouTube, my makeup is expertly applied. I never wore makeup at my old school, but I'd decided I would at the new one and Mom okay-ed it. Mom feels so guilty about us having to move away from our old school and everything we know that I think she'd okay just about anything right now. I run a finger over my new dangly star earrings. They look like tiny silver fireworks shooting from my earlobes. The earrings were a surprise gift from Mom for the first day of my new school. Sophie got a new soccer ball and shiny new pink Under Armour cleats.

There are still a few boxes scattered around, waiting for me to unpack, but for the most part, I've settled into my new bedroom. It's small and cramped and the walls are painted a really peculiar peach color that I absolutely hate, but Mom says we shouldn't repaint anything just now. She says it's only a rental and not our permanent home. We can choose our own wall colors when we move into the house we buy. Sophie is happy with her room, which is painted a cheery yellow. It has a great window seat with pillows that will make for a perfect homework spot. And it overlooks a great big weeping willow tree and a small hill that leads to a lake at the far end of the property. She was so miserable throughout the whole move that when I saw her perk up about the bedroom, I immediately backed down and let her have it. Hopefully my schedule will be so packed with all the great things I'll be doing with my new friends that I won't have time to sit around in my ugly room.

The last two weeks flew by. Mom and Dad were busy packing up the whole house and I was busy working on my popularity plan. I think I'm ready. I studied every page of the magazines Anusha had brought me. And I read every blog and article online about being popular and confident. I studied more for this first day of my new school than I did for my history final last year. I'm going to rock this.

My friends helped me so much too. Each time they found a great tip or piece of advice somewhere, they texted it to me. And we took pictures of my new clothes, and some pieces from my old wardrobe, and put together outfits. We made a look book, just like I'd seen girls do on reality shows, so now I won't have to think about what to pair together with what.

I must admit, though, that I worked the hardest on myself. On my mindset, that is. If this plan is going to work, I have to walk into my new school with a great attitude. I'm going to convince people that they *want* to be my friend. I need to act cool, so everyone thinks I'm cool. I didn't have the highest self-confidence at my old school, but everyone already knew me there. No one knows me at this school. I can let them believe I was the most popular kid in my entire school and they'll never know the difference.

"Taylor," Mom calls, "are you ready to go?"

I check myself in my mirror one more time. "You got this," I say to my reflection. To Mom I yell, "Coming!"

I grab my backpack and coat and race out to the driveway. Sophie is already riding shotgun in the car. I remind myself to be nice. Today is going to be hard on her.

I look at Mom and Sophie's faces as I climb into the backseat. Mom has her jaw clenched tight and I can see Sophie's eyes look red-rimmed. I bet she's already been crying this morning.

"All set," I say in the cheeriest voice I can manage. I am really excited about starting the new school, but I'm also a giant ball of nerves. What if I don't pull this thing off? What if I walk into the school and the kids take one look at me and somehow instantly know that I'm a total geek? Maybe there's nothing I can do to manipulate popularity and it's just something we're born with, like blonde hair or brown eyes?

Stop it, I scold myself. This kind of attitude is certainly not going to get me anywhere. An image of my friends sitting around the food court table fills my mind, and Nora saying, "Fake it 'til you make it." That's what I'm going to do. Even if I feel like the biggest loser to ever walk those junior high halls, I'm not going to let anyone else know that. I'm going to walk in like I'm the guest of honor.

I take another deep breath and straighten my back. I read in one of the online blogs that slouching wasn't for winners. Confident people walked with their backs straight and their heads held high.

I run two fingers along my friendship bracelet on my wrist as Mom drives down Main Street. Centerview really is a cute little town. There are fall decorations hung on storefronts and banners announcing the bicentennial hanging from lamp posts. We drive by a florist, a used bookstore, a coffee shop, and a really neat old-fashioned ice cream parlor. They're all within walking distance of the house we're renting, and I can almost see myself walking to town with my future great big group of friends this summer for a scoop.

"Do you have everything you need, Taylor? You

grabbed your lunch, phone, new gym clothes?" Mom asks.

"Yes, yes, and yes," I say.

"What about you, Soph? Got everything?"

"I suppose," Sophie replies, moodily.

"I can't wait to pick you up from school this afternoon and hear all about the amazing day you've had," Mom says.

Sophie sighs loudly, ignoring Mom's optimism, and leans her forehead against her window.

Poor Soph. She's really hating all this. I hope Mom's right and things do go well for her. I know I'm going to have an amazing day. I can't wait to get to school and get it started. "You're dropping me off first, right, Mom?"

"Yep, we're just about at your new school now." Mom pulls the car into a line of about thirty or so cars, inching slowly forward.

I frown to myself. This is going to take forever. "Can I get out and walk the rest of the way, Mom?"

Mom turns her head to look at me. "Really? Don't you want to wait for me to park? I can walk you in," she says.

"No!" I practically scream. My mom walking me

into school like a five-year-old definitely does *not* scream Miss Popularity. "I mean, I'll be fine. Really. It's a school. How hard is it to find the office and check in? I'm in seventh grade. Plus, I've already printed out my schedule. I'll be just fine by myself, and this way you'll have more time to help out Sophie at her school."

Sophie flips around in her seat and shoots me daggers with her eyes.

I shrug. I didn't mean to throw her under the bus, but this is pretty important. She'll understand when she's in junior high.

Mom bites her bottom lip while she thinks. She glances at Sophie, who has a full-on scowl now, and then back at me. "Well, if you really think you'll be okay . . ."

"I'll be great," I say, cutting her off. I lean into the front and kiss her on the cheek. "Thanks, Mom! Bye, Sophie!" I say as I let myself out of the car.

I start to walk quickly toward the front door and then I remember to slow down. I shouldn't burst into the school like it's the mall on Black Friday. I need to keep my head up, shoulders back, and casually stroll in like I own the place. Well, maybe not own it, but like I belong here and people should take notice of me.

I lift my chin and breezily walk into school, pausing to nod at a group of girls huddled around one of their iPhones.

This is going to be great.

Chapter Six
I'VE GOT THIS

Twenty minutes later, I've successfully mastered my new locker combination, unloaded my backpack, coat, and extra books, and I'm sitting in my first-period class: social studies with Mrs. Stevenson. Mrs. Stevenson is wearing a black top with a bright red skirt and over-the-knee black boots with really tall, skinny heels. She has her hair teased high and is wearing bright red lipstick with super long matching red nails that she likes to make clickety-clack on the desk as she talks. She reminds me of the realtor Dad hired to sell our house back home.

So far things are going pretty well. I'm acting super confident, smiling a lot, and maintaining eye contact. I'm trying to be kind, friendly, and approachable. All tips I picked up from a post on the TangoTeen website. When Mrs. Stevenson asked me to introduce myself to the class, I stood up, walked to the front of the room, and made sure to look at each person at least once as I talked. I reminded myself to slow down as I spoke and to use a powerful tone. And though it was super hard, I didn't say *like* or *uh* even once. I told the class I had moved from the city rather than just saying "a suburb of," because I thought it would make me sound more intriguing. And I think it's working because I can hear kids already buzzing about me. I keep my head held high and pretend not to notice.

I casually survey the kids in class to get a feel of who's who. Without even hearing them speak, I can tell who's the jokester, who the quiet ones are, the smart ones, who just wants to doodle in their notebook and be left alone, and who the popular kids are. I zeroed in on one particular student, Elle Jones, right away. She is tall, fit, and Disney Channel Star gorgeous with long shiny brown hair and giant green eyes that remind me of a Beanie Boo's. Well, maybe they're not that big, but they're definitely striking. I saw her in the hallway right before class started and noted the way the other girls hovered around her and hung on her every word like she was feeding them the answers to a test worth half their grade. And even now in class, while Mrs. Stevenson is talking, I can see several girls watching Elle's every move for clues as to how they should react and feel about everything going on in class. If she rolls her eyes, they roll their eyes back. If she smirks at something, they smirk too. It's strangely fascinating the power this particular popular girl has over her classmates. I must befriend her.

"This week, we're going to be doing a rather fun assignment to continue our study of the Roman Empire," Mrs. Stevenson tells the class.

"Yeah, right," a boy mumbles from behind me. A couple of other boys laugh softly.

Mrs. Stevenson either doesn't hear them or ignores them and continues on. "I want you to be explorers, traveling back in time to ancient Rome. You and a partner will create an online newspaper in which you describe in detail what you've learned so far. Since you are a newspaper, I expect you will have an article about a main event from history, but you may also include fun stuff like fashion, a comic, or interviews with a famous person from that time. You can even add Wanted Ads, obituaries, or advertisements. It's up to you what to include in your newspaper."

I know some people might not be too happy with the project, but it sounds kind of fun to me. My mind is already racing with ideas for a Dear Abby–type of column to include.

"Taylor," Mrs. Stevenson says, interrupting my thoughts, "I may have to come up with something else for you to do if you're not familiar with the subject."

"Oh no, that's okay," I assure her. "I can do the project. We actually just finished a unit on the Roman Empire at my old school."

She beams at me. "Fantastic. Well how about I pair you with . . ." She looks down and scans a list of names on a sheet she's holding and then looks back up. "Elle Jones. Elle, you don't mind helping out a new student, do you?"

Yes! I think to myself. This is perfect. I look at Elle and catch her roll her eyes slightly at one of her friends before smiling brightly at Mrs. Stevenson.

"Of course not," she says.

I flash her a grin. She might not be thrilled to work

with me yet, but I'll win her over. Mrs. Stevenson finishes pairing up the rest of the class and tells us to move desks so we can begin working on our projects.

I noticed Elle doesn't budge so I gather my stuff and make my way over to her. I can feel my muscles tense in anticipation of our conversation. I remind myself to be friendly, speak with confidence, and maintain eye contact.

"Hey, there," I say as I slip into a desk next to hers. I smile and wait for her to look at me.

She's scribbling something down in her notebook and doesn't look up. "Hey," she replies in a bored voice.

My mind is scrambling, trying to figure out what to say. I have to do something to draw her attention away from her notebook and up to me. And then it hits me. Flattery. One of the articles I read in Anusha's sister's magazine said to show interest in other people and try complimenting them. People love to be praised, and this is an easy way to get someone to like you. Bonus points if I can get her to talk about herself. People also seem to really like that. The trick is going to be not being too obvious. I quickly look Elle over and zone in on her outfit. It's nicely put together and looks like she put in a lot of effort to look good for school.

"I love your top." I say. "Hollister, right? I think I saw it last weekend when I was shopping with my friends. It's super cute." There. I was complimentary without going too overboard.

Elle looks down at her top, a soft gray with long, billowy sleeves, and then back to me. Her lips ease into a cautious smile. "Yeah. It is."

I see her gaze move over me, taking in my outfit. She gives an appreciative nod, and I'm totally beaming on the inside.

I worked hard on my first-day-of school outfit and practically drove my friends nuts with the countless pictures of combinations I texted to them. Everyone agreed, though, cuffed boyfriend jeans, chunky ankle boots, and, of course, a *lavender*, slouchy sweater was the perfect look to introduce the world, well, the Washington Junior High world, to the new me. I feel like one of the girls from the teen fashion blogs.

"Have you seen the sneak peek to the new spring line?" I ask her. "I guess camo is still a thing. I'm not sure I'm loving that." Really, I have no thoughts on camouflage either way. But I saw a fashion vlogger say that on You Tube and it sounded really cool.

"No, I didn't see it. We don't have a store anywhere nearby so my dad just orders online for me. Our shopping situation around here kinda stinks. Do you have a link?" she asks.

"Sure, I can text it to you."

"I'm so over camouflage, too," Elle adds with an eye roll. "It's like, enough already."

"I know, right?" I say.

Elle nods. "And at least once a year someone tries to bring back legwarmers."

"Oh, don't even get me started on legwarmers," I tell her as I widen my eyes, feigning my disgust, when really, I'm practically giddy on the inside. This is going so well! Elle and I are talking easily, and she already wants me to text her, which means she's going to give me her number which means I'm in. I hope.

Elle and I work on our project for the rest of the class and we seem to really click with our ideas. She loves the Dear Abby idea for the paper but thought we should come up with an authentic roman woman's name. Which I thought was a genius idea. So, we googled and decided on Dear Cornelia, after Pompey the Great's wife.

"The bell is going to ring in about two minutes," Mrs. Stevenson calls out. "Start gathering your things and straightening up your rows again."

"Here, give me your phone," Elle says, holding out her palm toward me.

I unlock my phone screen and hand her my phone.

She adds herself to my list of contacts and hands it back to me. "Do you have any plans for lunch?" she asks.

I almost want to laugh. Almost. What kind of lunch plans could I possibly have other than follow the herd of students to the cafeteria? But I hold it together. "Nothing set in stone," I reply, hoping that sounds good.

"Cool. Sit with me and my friends. You'll find us at one of the tables near the glass wall."

I want to jump up and down and take a victory lap around the classroom, fists pumping in the air. My plan is so totally working. A lunch invite from the "it" girl of the seventh grade? Things could not be working out any better. I can't wait to text Anusha, Nora, and Julie every last detail when I get home.

"Cool," I say, mimicking Elle's breezy tone. "I'll find you then."

The bell rings and we file out of the classroom. I exit ahead of Elle so she can't see me grinning like a fool.

chapter seven
It's Working!

"Hey, Taylor," Elle calls out from behind me as I make my way through the hall on the way to lunch. "Hold up."

I turn around and grin at her. "Hey, there." I say.

"I'll walk with you," she says and we resume our route to the cafeteria. A group of five really pretty girls suddenly appears and walks straight for us in the hallway. Elle looks up and dazzles them with a smile. "Hey, there," she says coolly to the group.

Normally, this kind of scene might cause me to start to panic but I follow Elle's lead. I plaster my best smile across my face and ask, "How's it going?"

The tallest of the girls gives me a quick onceover.

"Good, thanks," she says to me before turning her attention to Elle. "Listen, I was wondering if you wanted to be in on the spring dance planning committee. We won't start meeting until after winter break."

Elle shrugs like it's no big deal. "Sure, text me the details when you've got them. Taylor here will join, too, won't you?" she asks me.

"Of course," I reply and smile at the group of girls again. I have no clue what I'm agreeing to, but if Elle thinks I should do it, then I'm doing it.

I watch the small group study me like I'm a piece of a puzzle but they can't quite make out yet where I fit. "Sure," the tallest girl replies. "Great, I'll get you both down. Thanks, guys."

With that, the group of girls turns and continues down the hallway. Elle and I start off again, too.

"Dance committee is so fun," Elle tells me. "We get to pick the music, décor, everything."

"It sounds great," I reply in an equally cool voice to Elle's, but I'm squealing on the inside. The way Elle just so casually slipped me into this group of girls was amazing. I couldn't have picked a better person to be my first friend at this school.

We arrive in the noisy, chaotic cafeteria where lunch is already in full swing.

Elle grabs an empty chair from a nearby table and puts it next to her spot. "Here, sit by me, Taylor," she says, patting the back of the chair.

I smile and slip into the seat next to her at her lunch table. It's fifth period and there are already seven girls crammed around Elle's table. From the longing glances coming from nearby tables, if there were any more room, I'm sure more girls would like to cram in. I briefly wonder if I somehow surpassed someone in the hierarchy for my seat, being that Elle personally invited me to join their table. I slowly survey the situation and notice a couple of people at the adjacent tables with wounded looks discreetly checking me out. Oh well. I didn't mean to step on any toes. And I want everyone to like me, not just Elle and her friends. I shoot them a smile and nod. Which I think shocks one of the girls. Her eyes go wide like she got caught doing something she shouldn't. She recovers quickly, though, and smiles back.

I open my lunch bag, pull out a bottle of water, and take a sip. My morning has gone really well. This school is much smaller than my old school and the students have all been really nice and welcoming to me. The teachers have all been great too. In science, we did an experiment to figure out how glowsticks glow, and in Spanish, Senorita Muñoz let me do my introduction in Spanish only. I only just started taking Spanish this school year so all I said was my name is Taylor and I like the color pink. But she said it was *muy bueno*.

I turn my attention back to the group I've joined and, while they all seem like nice, pretty girls, I can see that just like this morning in social studies, they all watch Elle carefully. She's definitely the queen of this group.

A tiny girl named Shriya stabs at a yummy-smelling vegetarian curry as she eyes me. I'm feeling a bit of lunch envy as I have pretty basic chicken lettuce wraps for my main course. "So, Taylor," she starts in a tone that sounds more suspicious than interested, "what did you do for fun when you lived in the city?"

I swallow my bite of chicken wrap as I think. I don't think now is a great time to correct her and tell her I'm from a suburb of and not the actual city. They really are two completely different worlds. And I want to sound interesting so I can't exactly say I played

Minecraft at Nora's or walked to the public library with Julie. I clear my throat. "Oh, you know, movies, museums, and occasionally we'd see a play. My mom took us to the Art Institute at least once a month."

I take another bite of my wrap and watch the girls exchange looks as they take this in. We really did go to movies, local ones at the cineplex, and my parents did occasionally take us to the Chicago museums on the free days. I've never seen a play in the city, though. Mom and Dad had a few times and they'd gotten a babysitter for Sophie and me, but they'd never taken us along. Mom says tickets cost a fortune.

Vanessa, a tall girl with long black braids and the coolest interspersed dark purple braids, pipes in. "I went to the Art Institute last summer. My aunt took me and my cousins when I stayed with them for a week."

"Nice," I say. "Did you like it?"

Vanessa looks like she's mulling my question over. "Yeah. It was okay, I guess. Not as fun as the summer we went to the Museum of Science and Industry but it was still pretty good."

"Well, the science museum is the best. That's our favorite too. Followed by the Shedd Aquarium."

Vanessa nods. "Cool, I want to go there next."

Shriya glances at Elle, who is watching me carefully. I pretend like I don't notice.

"Do you miss it?" Lola, a pretty girl with thick dark hair and tawny beige skin, asks me. "I mean, the city, your old life, home, do you miss it?"

I think about this. There are some things I miss, like my old friends, my daily routine, and my old bedroom. But I'm with my family so, so far, it's all kind of seemed vacation-like to this point. "Um, some things," I tell her. "I haven't been gone long enough yet to miss it too much, I guess."

Shriya still looks at me like she doesn't trust me.

One of the other girls, Mackenzie, looks at me with genuine interest and not like I'm about to steal the lead in the school play from underneath her. I smile at her and she returns a friendly grin.

"Oh," I say suddenly, remembering the special treat I packed in my lunch, especially for the first day, and, the perfect reason to get all the attention off of me and onto something else, "do you guys like chocolate?" I pull out the large Toblerone bar from my lunch bag and set it on the table.

Most of the girls smile and nod emphatically.

I slide the foil-covered chocolate out of the

paper triangle package and rip it open. "Here, help yourselves."

The Toblerone was an impulse purchase when I was at the mall with Anusha, Julie, and Nora. We were browsing in a novelty store and a poster for sale caught my eye. It read, KILL 'EM WITH KINDNESS. OR CHOCOLATE. When I bought the candy, I was thinking if all else failed, everyone loves chocolate, so maybe I could win some friends that way.

"Yum!" Mackenzie says. "I love Toblerone."

"Me too," another girl, Gianna, agrees.

The girls slide the bar back and forth and even Elle breaks off a triangle and pops it in her mouth.

Just as Shriya passes the candy back to me, a clementine orange goes whizzing by my head.

"Sorry," I hear a male voice from behind me say.

I turn around in my seat and see a tall, good-looking boy grinning down at me. We briefly lock eyes, and I can feel myself begin to blush. He has big brown eyes and long-ish blonde hair that hangs down in the front, looking like it partly obstructs his vision. The sides and the back of his hair are shaved. He shakes his head to the left to knock the long hair out of his eyes.

"I was aiming for Huang over there," he says with a nod.

I follow his gaze and see a shorter boy with dark hair, holding the orange. He waves it at me.

"No harm," I tell him and then notice his eyes drift down to my candy bar. I hold it out to him. "Want a piece?"

"Yeah, sure," he says. He reaches toward the candy and breaks off a triangle.

His friend comes over and breaks off a piece too. "Thanks."

"Yeah, thanks," the first boy says and then they both keep walking toward what I'm guessing is their lunch table.

"Oh, my gosh," Gianna whispers from my right once the boys are out of earshot, "do you know who that was?"

I hear Elle clear her throat from my left. "No," I reply, hoping my cheeks aren't still pink.

"That was Daniel Thompson," Lola fills me in. "He's like, the hottest boy in the entire seventh grade."

I raise my eyebrows. He was pretty cute. Definitely cuter than any of the boys I knew from my old school.

"Maybe he likes you?" Mackenzie suggests.

I see Shriya shoot Elle a look.

"I doubt it," I say, quickly. "He probably just likes my candy bar."

"I don't know," Elle says, grinning at me. "I think Mackenzie might be right. He did give you a special kind of look there."

The girls are just being nice because I'm new. I'm sure of it. There is no way I'm hanging out with the popular girls and getting interest from the hottest boy in school on the first day. It's completely absurd. It's not even in the realm of possibilities. Things just don't change that quickly.

I break off a triangle of the Toblerone and let the smooth chocolate dissolve in my mouth. But what if it were true?

Chapter Eight
BUS EVACUATION DRILL DRAMA

I make my way from the locker room into the gym seventh period in my new gym uniform in the school colors, maroon and gold. Gyms have always made me a little nervous, maybe because I'm so uncoordinated. I always feel like I'm going to be terrible at whatever is the chosen sport of the week and that no one will pick me to be on their team. Being the last one standing as captains take turns choosing their teams is a thing of nightmares. But this is a new school, I remind myself, and no one knows how bad I am at every sport ever invented yet. I can just pretend like I know what I'm doing. At least until teams are chosen.

I look around the groups of students clustered together, waiting for the gym teacher to start the class. I spot Elle almost immediately and feel a whoosh of relief. She's sitting with two of the girls I met today at lunch. Lola and Gianna, I think they are. I make my way over to them.

"Yay, you're in gym with us," Elle says and pats the ground next to her.

I take a seat on the glossy hardwood floor. "I'm so glad. So, what have you guys been playing in here?" I ask, hoping for something easy like badminton or maybe archery.

"Square dancing," Gianna answers flatly. "It's a freaking nightmare."

I act aghast. "You're kidding."

"Unfortunately, not," Elle says. "But we won't be doing it today. It's bus evacuation drill day."

"Phew," I say, and mean it. I can handle evacuating a bus like a pro.

"We love bus evacuation drill day," Lola explains, "because it wastes like, the entire class period."

"And you can bring your phone," Gianna adds. "Everyone does. Mr. Walker doesn't even care."

"Great," I say. "Why did we have to change into our uniforms, though?"

"In case we get done early," Elle replies. "He'll make us jog or something."

"Ah." At least we all look the same in our uniforms. You wouldn't know who was popular or unpopular in the class. Although Elle has a natural sort of cool confidence that makes her stand out regardless of what she wears. I have to work harder on that.

After taking attendance, Mr. Walker, my new gym teacher, lets us all go back to the locker room to retrieve our coats (and phones) and then we all head outside and line up next to the big, yellow bus. It takes some time to move each group through the procedures so we have time to talk while we wait.

I'm standing behind Elle when Mr. Walker tells us to board and suddenly she's gone in a flash.

"Elle?" I say aloud and look around. Where did she go?

"Move it, Hunt," Mr. Walker says to me. "I know you're new but I'm sure you've done the drill before."

I look around one more time for Elle and then follow the boy in front of me onto the bus.

"Take the first available seat," the bus driver

bellows out. "Two to a seat, don't be picky. Keep it moving. We can't get started until everyone has taken a seat."

I reach the middle of the bus and slip into the seat with the boy who was in front of me, taking the aisle.

I watch the rest of the students file onto the bus and I finally spot Elle near the front, sitting with a dark-haired boy with huge dimples, and the likely reason for my abandonment back there. She motions for me to check my phone so I pull it out of my pocket and sure enough, there is a text from her. I had felt it vibrate a few moments ago but didn't want to check it in front of the teacher or bus driver. I read her text. It says, *OMG, I'm so sorry!!*

I give her a puzzled look and then send back, *???*

I see her typing furiously on her phone and a moment later her text reaches me. I read it and it says, *You're stuck with Colin Wright, EW! I'm soooooooooooooooooo sorry!* Then she sends a whole line of crying emojis.

I casually throw a sideways glance at the boy next to me, who must be Colin, and I'm not sure why she's so upset. What's wrong with him? Does he pick his nose and fling the boogers? Have bad breath?

What could warrant a dozen crying emojis? Sure, he isn't wearing the standard Under Armour trainers and color-coordinated hoodies and track pants that most of the other boys in our grade are wearing. Colin is sporting an insignia-free plain navy hoodie and sweatpants. And sure, the other boys all have perfectly coiffed hair that is supposed to look like it naturally sticks up this way and not that they spend twenty minutes in the mirror each morning putting it in place. Colin's hair looks like he has truly just rolled out of bed. It kind of reminded me of this girl named Jeanie that I knew in elementary school. She never brushed her hair. Her mom made her keep it really short since she wouldn't take care of it. Colin's hair really isn't even that bad. The curls hanging down his forehead and into his eyes are even sort of sweet. What could Elle find so offensive about him?

My phone dings again with another text from Elle. I take a deep breath and look down.

Total Freakshow! she wrote.

Okay, so Elle really dislikes this kid. Which probably means he's not in her crowd and not someone I should be associating with. But what's the big deal?

It's just a bus evacuation drill. It will be over soon enough.

Another text from Elle comes in and I feel the hairs on the back of my neck prickle. It says, *Switch seats.*

I scowl and casually look around the bus. Every seat is taken and there is no way I could switch even if I wanted to. Elle is being ridiculous. And super rude. If I were back at my old school and someone was acting like this, I'd give them an earful. Then again, I wasn't popular at my old school. I'm at my new school and trying desperately to fit in with the popular crowd, a.k.a., Elle. Which means I can't exactly school her on kindness.

I bite my bottom lip and try to think of what to reply. I type, *I'm stuck!* and send back three screaming emojis. I truly don't care about sitting by Colin but what else can I do?

I look up and see Elle looking at me sympathetically. I roll my eyes and curl the corner of my lip in a disgusted look. Like I'm really put out with my current circumstances.

A wave of dread comes over me, and I hope Colin did not just see me do that. I'll feel completely awful if I hurt his feelings. I risk a peek at him and he's looking out the window. I breathe a sigh of relief.

As I'm about to face back forward, Colin turns his head and catches me looking at him. That's just great. I practically slam my phone into my chest, not wanting him to read what Elle and I have been texting to each other. He gives me a curious look, and I smile brightly at him. He's probably a perfectly nice boy and Elle is just being dramatic.

He raises one eyebrow at me and then turns back toward the window to stare outside again.

My phone alerts me to yet another text from Elle. I slowly pull it away from my chest and read. It says, *I owe you!*

Chapter Nine

Group Texting with the Popular Girls

Vanessa: Blech. Sushi again.

Mackenzie: Yum! I love sushi!

Vanessa: Not at my house you wouldn't. My mom makes it herself. *shudder*

Mackenzie: I can see how that might go south. 😊

Lola: My abuela is cooking . . . YUM.

Taylor: Lucky you!

Gianna: Your grandma's food rocks.

Elle: We have a meal delivery service. I don't know what it is tonight.

Shriya: Hey, did you guys hear about what happened in our gym class? During bus evacuation?

Vanessa: omg, yes! It was intense!

Lola: No, what?

Taylor: ???

Shriya: Armani Brown and Renatta Cruz got into a screaming match. The bus driver threw them off the bus before the drill even got started.

Mackenzie: Why? What happened?

Vanessa: Renatta hit like on a pic Armani's boyfriend put up on his Insta.

Gianna: So?

Shriya: Armani didn't think she should do that I guess.

Lola: Srsly? Omg.

Taylor: That's weak.

Mackenzie: For real. Who cares?

Elle: We had drama at bus evac today too. Taylor was such a star, tho.

Vanessa: What happened?

Elle: She got stuck in a seat with Colin! Ick.

I cringe as I read Elle's text. Why does she have to make this such a big deal? I wish she'd just let it go. Now I have to say something.

Shriya: Oh no, Taylor!!!

Vanessa: And on your first day. Poor thing.

Taylor: It was okay. I washed with antibacterial soap right after. Twice.

Elle: ☺

Shiya: hahahaha!

Vanessa: lol

I smile sadly at my phone. I'm glad I could make the others laugh, but I don't feel good about typing that. It's so mean. And completely untrue. Colin actually seems like an okay guy. We never spoke during the bus evacuation drill, but when I got to eighth-period honors math today, he was there. It's a small class, only a dozen kids total, and the only empty seat was at the two-person table with Colin. It crossed my mind that I should try to secure alternative seating after Elle's earlier reaction to Colin, but I looked around the room and didn't see anyone from Elle's group in there—or anyone who might possibly talk to someone from Elle's group—so I figured it was okay. Besides, it wasn't like I could demand the teacher make another student move because my new friend Elle dislikes Colin. So, I sat down with him. I even tried to be funny. I said, "Hey, there, bus seat buddy." He sorta smiled at me, probably not knowing how to take me. As the class went on, I discovered that who we sit with is who we partner with for group work in class. Colin and I completed a sheet of math problems together, and he seems pretty smart from what I can tell. He's nice too. He even offered to let me make a copy of his notes. Before we left class today, the teacher told Colin and me to exchange phone numbers so I could reach out to him outside of the school day for help if I needed it. It's kind of funny that I have both Elle and Colin's numbers saved in my phone. Elle would totally freak out about that.

"Taylor?" Mom says, pushing my door open and letting herself into my room.

I quickly drop my phone face down on my bed and pull a notebook into my lap so it would look like I was doing homework. "Yeah?"

"I thought we'd order out from that pizza place downtown to celebrate you and Sophie have such great first days. What do you feel like getting?"

I smile. I love pizza, and I definitely feel like celebrating. "Can we get double pepperoni?"

"Sure, double pepperoni for you and sausage for Soph. It'll be about thirty minutes." Mom moves to leave and then pauses. She turns back to look at me. "I'm so glad it went well today, Tay. Think you're going to like it here?"

I nod emphatically. "I really do, Mom."

Mom smiles, clearly feeling relief. Today was probably stressful on her too. Sophie had her a nervous wreck all for nothing. She had a great first day and has been talking about her new friend Molly all afternoon. Sophie got into a black-top soccer game at recess with Molly and a few of the other girls against a big group of fifth grade boys and the girls kicked their butts. Sophie scored three of their goals herself.

Mom walks out of my room and closes the door behind her.

I pick up my phone and start reading. Things are going even better than Mom thinks. I can't believe I'm group texting with the popular girls! And on my first day of school. It's insane. I need to text my friends back home and fill them in on what's happened today. They're never going to believe it.

Taylor: You guys, guess who I'm group texting with RIGHT NOW.

Anusha: Us?

Taylor: 😊 Well, yes, of course. But I mean in another text.

Nora: Your mom?

Taylor: Oh geez, I'll just tell you. The most popular girls in the entire 7th grade at Washington Junior High!!!!!

Anusha: Really? No way!

Nora: Wow! So, the plan is working?

Taylor: Like a dream! Where's Julie? She's not replying.

Nora: Skating.

Taylor: Oh. Anyway, YES! I hit it off with their like, queen, first thing this morning and she pulled me into the group. I'm still pinching myself.

Anusha: I'm impressed. I wasn't sure it was going to work.

Taylor: Why? Because I'm terminally uncool?

Anusha: 🙁 No, of course not!

Nora: That's not what she meant, Taylor. We're happy for you that the plan is working so well so quickly.

Anusha: Yes! It's awesome, congrats!

Taylor: Well, I have to be really careful and not screw up. It's hard. I almost said the wrong thing a couple of times today.

Nora: Like what?

Taylor: Nothing really. Just have to be careful. I better go so I can concentrate on my other group text. Talk soon.

I click back over the texts with Elle and the rest of the girls and I'm a bit behind and have to catch up on the conversation. I'm a little bummed my back-home friends weren't more excited for me. Especially since they helped me so much with my plan. I thought they'd be thrilled things were working out so well. Then again, maybe I'm reading too much into it. They did say they were happy. Sometimes it's hard for emotion to come across clearly in texts. Which is why I didn't tell them about the Daniel thing at lunch because I'm not sure there even really is a Daniel thing. And why I especially didn't tell them about what happened during the bus evacuation drill with Colin and Elle. I didn't want to shine a bad light on the new group I've joined. My friends never would have understood the position I was in. I felt bad about going along with Elle on the bus and again just now in picking on Colin in our text with my mean comment. But what am I supposed to do? I can fall out with these girls just as easily as I fell in. If I want to hang out with them, I have to behave and respond in a certain way. Speaking of which, I better jump back into the chat.

Taylor: Sorry guys, my mom was just in my room talking to me. I'm back! What did I miss?

Chapter Ten

S-P-I-R-I-T, WHO HAS SPIRIT? ME?

"I can't believe it's already Thursday," I say to Elle as I move my desk next to hers. It feels like this first week at the new school has just flown by and I've already settled into a comfortable routine. I like my teachers and I like my classes. And I found a huge, cool group of kids to hang out with just like I'd wanted. I haven't once worried about who I'd eat lunch with or who I'd partner with in gym and it feels really great.

Mrs. Stevenson just asked us to all move into our groups to continue working on our Roman Empire project. Elle already has her Chromebook open and our online newspaper pulled up. It's looking really good.

Today, Mrs. Stevenson is wearing a slim, dark purple dress, a chunky gold necklace, big gold and diamond rings, three on each hand, and gold high heels. Her nails are even painted a coordinating gold color. I love how she puts so much effort into her look each day. I bet she spends as much time preparing her outfit each night as I do. Probably even more.

"I need the weekend, like now," Elle says. She's staring at the screen and clicking through the pages of our paper.

"Tell me about it," I agree, even though I really don't mean it. I have no plans for the weekend other than to finish unpacking. Maybe I'll decorate my room a little.

Elle is editing the "interview" she did with Titus, the roman emperor from 79 to 81 AD, about the opening of the Colosseum and the challenges he's faced since succeeding his dad, Vespasian, while I'm working on an advertisement for an upcoming gladiator game, highlighting the special reserved seats in the awning-covered section with all of the meat and drinks any Roman could want.

A girl with bright red hair pulled back into a high pony tail and stylish blue eyeglasses stops next to Elle and looks at her Chromebook screen over her shoulder. "Wow," she says brightly. "That looks awesome! I bet you guys will have the best newspaper in the entire class."

"Probably," Elle replies flatly without taking her eyes off the screen.

The girl waits for a beat longer, hoping for some sort of further acknowledgment from Elle I'm guessing, before letting her shoulders droop and trudging back to her seat in the classroom.

Honestly, I'm a little surprised at the coldness Elle just displayed. She didn't give that girl the time of day. I casually glance over to the girl and she's still looking at Elle, sort of longingly and with a pouty expression. It's so weird! If it were me at my old school and a girl just acted rudely like that to me, I probably would have just thought *jerk*, and not bothered with her again. But the redhead girl looks super bummed and like it would make her day if Elle even smiled at her. The more Elle pays her no attention, the more she wants her attention. I'm completely fascinated by the power Elle Jones has.

And thankful once again that I've gotten myself in with her.

Elle scrolls through the page in front of her and adds in a few words to it. Suddenly, she flips her attention my way and smiles brightly. "Are you going to cheerleading tryouts after school tomorrow afternoon?"

My mind goes blank. Cheerleading? Had she mentioned this before? No, I'm sure I'd remember if she had. "Cheering for what? I mean, whom?" I ask. I'm pretty sure football is over by now. At least it was back home. I think.

"Basketball, of course," Elle replies. She turns in her chair to completely face me and puts a hand on my forearm. "You *have* to try out for cheerleading, Taylor. We all are."

I scramble for words. Why would I want to cheer for basketball? I hate basketball. Would that I mean I'd have to watch the games? And who is *we all*? Like, all of our friends? Is everyone into cheerleading? "You are?" I say, trying desperately to keep the panic out of my voice.

"Definitely. It's so much fun. We practice every day after school and make up killer dance routines. We pair up with the eighth-grade girls and do a fun little sister/big sister thing where we decorate each other's lockers on each game day. Everyone in school knows who the cheerleaders are. It's a great activity for you to join, especially since you're new."

That part does sound like fun, and I'd hate to miss out on valuable bonding time with the other girls, but I'm having a hard time envisioning the actual cheering portion of the activity as being fun. I'm so uncoordinated and I'd never be able to do all those cheer-y jumps and kicks cheerleaders are supposed to do. If I was going to participate in an after-school activity, I'd be better equipped for something like the math team. A mathlete is the only kind of "lete" I'm qualified for. There should be cheerleaders cheering for that. The equation I nailed in my homework last night deserved a back flip or two.

But I suppose my new friends wouldn't think the math team was the coolest group in the world to join. Actually, I'm pretty sure that Elle would fill my phone with puking emojis if I even mentioned it. I don't know what to say. "Um . . ." I stall.

"Taylor," Elle says, cutting me off, her voice more serious now. "you just *have* to try out. Daniel is on the basketball team. You'd be cheering for him," she adds, letting her voice sing a little on the word *him*.

"Oh, well, yeah. That would be amazing," I lie. Not that cheering for Daniel would be a bad thing; I would like to support him. And when I think back to the pep rallies at my old junior high and watching the cheerleaders doing their thing on the gym floor, I did always think how nice it must have been to feel special like that. To have all eyes on you and know that a good portion of the girls in the stands wished that they were you. If I do this, I'd get to experience how that felt. I really would be one of "them." But, on the other hand, I'm seriously starting to sweat envisioning myself doing cartwheels across the gym. I've tried a cartwheel before and it wasn't cute. My summersault isn't half bad though. Do cheerleaders summersault?

"Okay," Elle starts, "I was going to text you later about this, but . . ." She pauses and looks left and right to make sure no one else in class can overhear her.

I lean in closer.

She lowers her voice. "I don't know for one hundred percent sure, but I think Daniel likes you."

"What?" I practically squeal. Daniel Thompson

likes me? How is that even possible? No boy has ever liked me before. Especially not such a cute boy. The cute boys always like the most popular girls, not girls like me.

But wait. I'm not girls like me anymore, am I?

"Shh!" Elle scolds. She casually looks around to see if anyone has overheard.

I mentally scold myself on my uncool reaction just now. I need to chill. And act like cute boys liking me happens all the time. I lean in again and whisper in a much calmer tone, "What makes you think that?"

"I have English class with Brayden Hill who is like, Daniel's best friend since second grade. He asked me if you had a boyfriend and I told him, no, I didn't think so. You don't, right?" Elle asks.

Do. Not. Laugh. Hysterically, I tell myself. I'm a cool girl: smart, confident, *popular*. I could totally have had a boyfriend at my old school. True, it never ever happened, but it's one-hundred percent plausible, at least to my new friends. I just have to come up with something clever to say. "No," I reply. "I mean, I was sort of talking to this one guy at the start of the school year but we never actually dated or anything."

I can't believe I just said that. It was such a total lie!

There were a couple of kids in my seventh grade back home that were rumored to be "dating" someone but they sure weren't me. No one has ever taken an interest in me. Until now.

Wow. Daniel Thompson likes me. This is wild.

The eighth-period second bell rings just as I slide into my seat next to Colin, and I let out a huge happy sigh. Math is my favorite class. I love it for so many reasons. For one, I'm pretty darn good at it. Equations have always come easy for me and I find them fun. Numbers just make sense. In English we're constantly trying to figure out the meaning of things and in science we're always trying to discover and test stuff to see what reaction we get, but in math there is always a clear answer. I remember always liking math but I didn't know I was really good at it until third grade when I tested into honors math. Before that, I was sometimes self-conscious because I always knew the answers and I thought it made me stand out from the other kids. But in honors, all the kids know the answers and love math as much as me so it's fun.

I also love this class because I can breathe in

here. It's the last class of the day, and I can finally relax and be myself. Not that I would ever complain out loud, but being popular is hard work. I always have to watch what I say and do. My mind races all day, analyzing every situation I'm in and I'm constantly watching Elle and her friends for cues on how to act. It's exhausting. And getting ready in the mornings is literally taking twice as long as it used to take me back home. But I do really like how I look each day and it really is fun being popular so it's all worth it.

My eyes wander over to Colin, who's busy doodling on his notebook. I notice he has another book underneath his notebook that says, Dragon Master Guide.

"Hey, you into D&D?" I ask.

A subtle look of embarrassment crosses his face and his jaw stiffens. "Yeah, I play with my friends," he replies in a slightly defensiveness tone.

"Cool, me too," I say, unable to mask the excitement in my voice.

He arches one eyebrow at me.

"I mean, I did play before we moved here. My friends and I would play for hours when we had sleepovers."

Colin still looks at me like he doesn't believe me or he thinks I'm lying. "Really?" he asks.

"Well, it wasn't like we were being invited to all the after-football game parties," I joke.

Now Colin really is looking at me like I'm crazy.

I briefly close my eyes and frown, mentally face-palming myself. I suddenly remember that was the old me. The new me would have been invited to all the big after-game parties. The new me wouldn't have had time to play D&D. I bite my bottom lip and my mind races, trying to think of a way to talk myself out of this situation.

"I mean," I start, "I just think that it's cool that you play. Seems fun."

Colin shrugs. "Thanks, I guess."

It suddenly occurs to me that I don't know who Colin's friends are. I only ever see him in math and gym. In math he mostly just talks to me and in gym he doesn't really hang around with anyone. "Hey," I ask, before I can change my mind. "Who are the friends you play D&D with?"

I can see Colin studying me, probably wondering why I want to know this information. But I'm just curious to know more about him.

"Steven Chung and Owen MacIntyre," he replies.

"Oh, yeah, I know them," I say with a smile. Steven is from my science class; he's really smart and sort of quiet. And I have Spanish with the other boy, Owen. He's loud and goofy but also kind of funny. Both of them seem nice.

Colin smiles briefly at me and then looks back down at his notebook.

I think I sort of confuse him.

Mr. Martinez begins class and I pull out my own notebook to take notes. He's going over bivariate data using hot chocolate sales versus the temperature that day as the two variables.

I glance over at Colin again and he smiles back again, warmer this time. I'm creating a graph in my notebook to input the data Mr. Martinez is rattling off and Colin leans toward me and whispers.

"I think I'd understand this better if he provided samples."

I grin. "Yum. With marshmallows?

"Definitely."

"Mr. Walker, Ms. Hunt," Mr. Martinez says, "is my lecture interrupting your conversation?"

My eyes widen and I slink down a bit in my seat.

Colin shakes his head no.

"Sorry," I say.

Mr. Martinez resumes his lesson and Colin and I stifle giggles.

Chapter Eleven
NO, SHE DIDN'T!

The final bell rings and I gather my books. Colin gathers his too and we both move toward the door.

"Mr. Martinez sure lays on the homework, huh? Five sheets in one night is rough," I say to him.

"Yeah, he always does that. And I love how he phrases it like he's taking it easy on us. 'I know you guys have other classes and a life outside of school so I'll only give you nine thousand math problems for homework tonight,'" he jokes.

I laugh as we both squeeze out of the doorway at the same time.

"At least tonight's problems look pretty easy though," I tell him.

Colin opens his mouth to reply but before he can get anything out, Elle is in front of us.

"Later, Loser," she says loudly to Colin and then wraps a hand around my wrist and tugs.

I stumble toward her and my mouth drops open. I'm so shocked. Did she really just say that to Colin? Right to his face like that? That was so completely horrible.

I know I should say something, pry her hand off me or yell at her or really anything, but I don't know what to do. My neck feels hot and I'm filled with a sense of panic.

Elle is starting to pull me down the hall and I turn my head and look at Colin.

He's staring at me with a sad look on his face.

I'm not going to lie; it crushes me a little. "I'm sorry," I mouth to him. It's not the best thing to do, I know, but it's all I can think of right this moment.

I see Colin cast his eyes downward and then I turn back to face the direction Elle is pulling me. I'm furious and I want to scream at her, but I don't. I can't. I remind myself that screaming at the queen bee in the middle of the seventh-grade hallway would only earn me a one-way ticket out of the popular group. And I only just got here. So, I say nothing.

I'm lying on my stomach on my bed, my legs casually kicking at my bedroom wall, and my Chromebook perched in front of me. I've been watching YouTube videos full of cheerleading tips for the past hour and alternating back and forth between sheer terror and thinking maybe I can do this. I've learned about keeping my arm motions sharp and looking excited. I'm pretty sure that I can nail the excitement part. After all, it's just more pretending and I've been doing a great job with that. It's the flipping stuff I have no chance at. Elle told me not to worry about that part too much. We'll be cheering in the gym and there isn't enough space to do that kind of thing during an actual basketball game. I do need to work on jumps though so I'm watching tutorials and then practicing them in front of the bathroom mirror. And while I don't look like any of the girls in the YouTube tutorials, I'm at least getting off the ground.

My phone dings that I have a new text and I check it. It's Nora.

Nora: Hey!

Taylor: Hey you!

Nora: What are you up to? I miss you!

Taylor: I miss you too! And you wouldn't believe it if I told you.

Nora: Intrigued. Do tell.

Taylor: I'm YouTubing cheerleading videos.

Nora: Tay? I think my phone has a virus. It looks like you said you were YouTubing cheerleading videos.

Taylor: 😊 I did!

Nora: Why on earth would you do that?

Taylor: I'm trying out for cheerleading tomorrow after school.

Nora: WHAT?!

Taylor: Yup!

Nora: But you hate sports!

Taylor: True

Nora: And remember when we were trying to do the Cupid Shuffle at the sixth-grade dance? You practically sprained your ankle.

Taylor: Ugh. Don't remind me! I have zero coordination.

Nora: So, how are you going to be a cheerleader?

Taylor: I'm not sure. I'm going to try out though. All of my friends are doing it.

Nora: Wow! Well, good luck and please don't hurt yourself.

Taylor: 😊 I'll try not to. How was your day?

Nora: Same old, same old. I got a C on my science test so I'm stressing over that. I don't want my mom to find out.

Taylor: Aw, I'm sorry. Can you do any extra credit?

Nora: Maybe.

Taylor: I'm stressing too. Not school work-related though.

Nora: What's wrong?

Taylor: It's a long story. Got a minute? I'll call you.

Nora: Sure.

I sit up on my bed and close my Chromebook. I've been feeling bad ever since school ended today and maybe talking to Nora will help. I scroll through my contact list until I find her name and click on her phone number.

She picks up on the first ring. "Hey, what's going on?"

As soon as I hear Nora's voice, I can feel myself get choked up, like I might cry or something. Which is silly. Nothing is going that wrong to warrant tears. Most everything is going really well. Great, in fact. I think I just miss my friend. I take a deep breath. "It's nothing really horrible or anything. I just feel bad about something that happened at the end of school today."

"What happened?" Nora asks.

"Well," I begin, wanting to carefully choose my words. I don't want Nora to think my new friends aren't as great as I think they are, "you know my new friend Elle? She has really strong opinions about things and people."

"Yeah," Nora says.

"I'm in honors math last period and I sit by this nice boy named Colin. We work pretty well together. And he's pretty funny. We joke around and stuff."

"Okay . . ." Nora prompts.

"Elle sort of hates him. I'm not sure why, but she says a lot of mean things about him. Anyway, Colin and I were walking out of class together today, chatting and laughing about something, and Elle suddenly appeared in front of us and said, 'Later Loser,' to him and then snatched me away."

"Oh my gosh," Nora says, sounding horrified. "That's so rude."

"Yeah," I agree sadly, "I know. It was kind of awful. I could tell his feelings were hurt."

"Of course, they were. What's wrong with her?"

I instantly feel defensive of Elle even though technically I know her actions are indefensible. "Well, I don't think there's something necessarily wrong with her; she just really doesn't like him. Maybe he kicked her puppy or something and I just don't know about it."

"Really?" Nora says skeptically.

"I don't know. I'm mad at myself though. I should have done or said something right then and there instead of just walking off with Elle."

"Did you apologize to Colin?" she asks.

"Sort of," I say, thinking about how I mouthed an apology to him. "I texted him a funny math meme a little while ago. The teacher in it looked just like our math teacher, Mr. Martinez. But he didn't respond."

"You should definitely apologize again," Nora reiterates. "You said he was your math partner, right? You have to work with him all year. It wasn't your fault what your friend did but you don't want him to think you're that kind of person too."

"Yeah," I agree. "I know you're right."

"Don't beat yourself up too much, Taylor. Just talk to Colin tomorrow, and I'm sure he'll forgive you."

"I hope so."

Chapter Twelve
THE TRYOUTS

I take a sip from my water bottle before walking into math. My mouth is really dry and my hands are sweaty and gross. I've been nervous about having to face Colin all day. I already know he's not happy with me. We were square dancing in gym earlier and he wouldn't even make eye contact with me when we had to do-si-do. I tried to make a joke when he had to swing me 'round and 'round and promenade me back home but he didn't crack a smile. He's definitely mad. And I don't blame him one bit. Elle was horrible to him, and I'm associated with her. He probably thinks we share the exact same feelings about him. Elle, of course, made faces at me when I had to dance with Colin, but I ignored her. I wasn't letting her get me into further trouble with him. Besides, the gym teacher makes us switch partners a lot and Elle had to take a turn with Colin herself. I'm sure he hated that just as much as she did.

I slip into my seat next to Colin. He's hunched over his end of our table, scribbling in his notebook. I clear my throat and wait for him to look up, make eye contact, anything. But he doesn't move. I stack my books in a neat pile in front of me and look around the room. The second bell hasn't rung yet so people are still talking at their tables. We can't go on forever like this. I have to say something to fix it.

"So," I begin, trying to keep my voice light and friendly, "what are you working on there?" I look at Colin, expectantly. But he still doesn't look up. He stays completely focused on what he's writing. I sigh and look around the room again. Class is going to start any moment and we can't work together if we're not talking. I have to get him to look at me. I reach over and tap my pencil on his notebook.

Colin slowly lifts his head and looks at me. He's not smiling.

"How's it going?" I ask.

He shrugs a reply and starts to turn his attention back toward his notebook.

"Wait," I say, putting a hand lightly on his arm.

He looks down at my hand and then at me.

I quickly pull it back. "I just wanted to talk to you about yesterday. I'm sorry Elle was such a jerk to you."

He blinks a couple times and a flash of pain crosses his eyes. I can tell it had hurt his feelings and I instantly feel bad all over again.

"You should just ignore her though," I continue. "She doesn't know any better."

He gives me a quizzical look.

I lean in and lower my voice. "She was raised by howler monkeys. They're not known for manners. Her people pick bugs off each other's backs and fling their poop." I actually don't know anything about Elle's family, but I'm guessing she'd missed every single lesson on kindness in preschool.

A smile slowly spreads across Colin's face.

I smile back. I think he's going to forgive me.

I don't want to harp on the whole Elle thing so I quickly switch the subject. "Were you able to finish number fifteen on last night's homework? I think mine might be wrong. Can we compare?"

"Yeah," Colin says, finally breaking the silent treatment he had been giving me. He reaches into his binder and pulls out the assignment and sets a pack of gum on top of it. He pushes it toward me. "Want a piece?" he asks.

"Sure," I reply brightly. Relief fills me. Everything is going to be okay.

It's after school and I'm sitting on the gym floor with about forty other girls, a mix of seventh and eighth graders, stretching. I'm not entirely sure what I'm doing here so I'm just mimicking everything Mackenzie does. My legs are spread out in a V and I reach as far as I can toward my toes on my right foot and then switch and do the same toward my toes on my left foot. I stretch one arm overhead, grabbing my elbow, and then do the same with the opposite arm. So far things are going fine. I'm not sure what will happen once we actually start tryouts.

I look around for Elle and spot her talking to a few girls I don't know. "Who's Elle with?" I ask Mackenzie.

Mackenzie turns her head to look at Elle. "Oh, those are a couple of the eighth graders. The one with the long copper braids and nose ring is the eighth-grade cheer captain. Elle will be ours."

I narrow my eyes at Mackenzie. "How do you know?"

Mackenzie rolls her eyes and grins at me. "Just wait."

I smile back at Mackenzie and feel a new, special kinship with her. Does she also not think Elle is as great as everyone else in the school seems to think she is? Not that I necessarily think she's a bad person. Sure, I've witnessed her make some bad choices, but she did befriend me on the very first day of school. Elle already had everything she could want. She's the most popular girl in our grade. She didn't have to be nice to me and welcome me into her group but she did and for that, I'm grateful.

Mackenzie looks upward, over my head, and plasters a huge smile on her face.

I turn and look. "Hey, Elle," I say a little too quickly and maybe a bit guiltily since she had almost caught us talking about her.

Elle sits on the floor between Mackenzie and me and holds her phone out, high in the air above her head, and aims it downward. She tilts her face up and smiles as she snaps a selfie. She quickly uploads the photo to her Instagram and I see her label it #cheer #tryouts.

I briefly wonder if I should pull out my phone and do the same. But then I remember I left it in my backpack, clear across the gym. My friends back home and I were never big into selfies, but a lot of the girls take them here. And everyone is on Instagram. I'll need to make a concerted effort to start snapping and posting more.

Elle sets her phone down on the ground between us and puts her legs straight out in front of her. She reaches as far as she can with her hands, keeping her neck straight so that she's facing down. Her fingertips go a good six inches past her toes. She must be super flexible. I can't even reach my toes.

"Half of these people here are a joke," she says, still holding the stretch.

Mackenzie and I exchange a look over Elle's back.

"What do you mean?" Mackenzie asks.

I'm curious, too, because if she thinks these girls are a joke, then I'm an entire sitcom. Every single girl here looks like she knows what she's doing way more than I do.

Elle sits up and pulls one knee toward her chest.

"You see Jessie over there? She has zero coordination. And Trista has the voice of a mouse. No one would ever even know she was cheering unless she used a microphone."

Oh boy. I have a big mouth but my coordination is terrible. Elle is going to be saying this stuff about me in ten minutes.

"Weren't you and Jessie friends?" Mackenzie asks Elle.

My eyebrows rise. Friends? This should be interesting.

"Maybe in the distant past but not now," Elle says. "I would never be friends with such a loser."

I half frown. There's that word again. Elle is awfully fond of labeling people she doesn't like as losers. I wonder what Jessie did to fall out of Elle's circle? And I hope that whatever it is, I don't make the same mistake.

"She and Trista are wasting their time," Elle continues. "They're *not* going to make the team."

"But we haven't even tried out yet," I blurt out and instantly want the snatch the words right back. I hope Elle doesn't think I was challenging her. I should have just kept quiet.

Elle looks at me and grins. "Wait and see," she says and then gets to her feet and troops off toward the cheer sponsor, Mrs. Black.

I look at Mackenzie and she smirks. I lower my voice and say, "If she thinks those girls are uncoordinated, she's going to flip when she sees me. I can't even do a cartwheel."

"Don't worry," Mackenzie assures me, "Elle has pull with Mrs. Black. She'll make sure you get in."

I follow Mackenzie's gaze back to where Elle and Mrs. Black are standing. Elle looks like she's talking a mile a minute and Mrs. Black is laughing at whatever she's saying. Now she's nodding vigorously and looking at Elle with that same star-struck look a lot of the girls give her. Which is sort of freaking me out, and I would never believe it if I wasn't seeing it firsthand. Elle and Mrs. Black share a conspiratorial look and then Mrs. Black turns to face the group.

"All right girls, let's get these tryouts going. Everyone on your feet."

Chapter Thirteen
MAKING THE TEAM

It is mind-blowing the amount of pull Elle Jones has in this school.

I somehow made the cheerleading team.

It makes absolutely no sense. Like, zero. I may not have been the worst cheerleader that Washington Junior High has ever seen but I most certainly was the worst one at tryouts. I mean, I know this for a fact and so do the rest of the girls that were at that tryout. I did give it my all: I was as articulate as I could be, I injected as much passion into my words and movements as possible, and I smiled like it was Christmas morning and I had just received a pony. But the other girls were just flat out better. They could do complicated jumps, kick higher, and in general just move their bodies in a more superior way than I could. Yet, ten other girls were cut and I made the seventh-grade cheerleading squad. I'm doing it. I'm going to be one of the popular girls, cheering on the basketball court. Girls will watch me with envy and wish they were me. And it's all thanks to Elle.

"Are you so excited?" Elle asks, sidling up next to me in front of the cheer team announcement posted on the bulletin board outside of the gym.

I turn toward her, grab both of her hands, and jump up and down. "I'm so so so so excited!" I squeal, completely giddy. I've almost shocked myself with how pumped I am.

Elle laughs and jumps with me for a few seconds and then wraps her arms around my neck for a quick hug. She pulls away and nods back at the list. "Did you see I'm the captain?"

I turn back to the board and scan the list again until I reach the bottom. There it says, *Seventh-Grade Cheer Captain: Elle Jones.* "Oh my gosh, Elle! Congratulations! You totally deserve it! You were so *amazing* at tryouts, it was completely inspirational, and you'll make the best leader, hands down." Okay,

I'm laying it on a little thick. Maybe I should rein it back just a bit. I subtly glance around to see if anyone else was nearby and overheard my gushing. I'd be kind of embarrassed if Mackenzie had heard me go on like that.

"Thanks, Taylor," Elle replies, seeming truly touched by my praise. "Did you see all our friends made it too? Mackenzie, Vanessa, Gianna, everyone. It's going to be so much fun. We're going to have the best time."

I run my eyes over the list again and sure enough, our entire lunch table is listed. And there's my name again. Taylor Hunt. I really made the cheerleading squad. I pull out my phone and snap a quick pic of the list. I'm sure I'll look at it again and again just to make sure it really happened. I couldn't wipe the grin from my face if I wanted to. Sure, the concept of cheerleading, at first, seemed kinda weird, and it wasn't something I'd ever wanted to do before, but it's like crossing the finish line into popularity. I'm here. I made it. I'm really going to be a cheerleader and with a great big group of friends. Oh wow, I can't wait to get home and tell my mom and dad and Sophie. I've got to text my back-home friends too.

Anusha, Julie, and Nora are never going to believe this.

"Can you stay after school today?" Elle says, interrupting my thoughts.

"Hmm?" I ask, feeling like I missed something. My eyes flick over to meet hers.

"After school," Elle repeats. "They whole squad is going to stay after and hang out at the boys' basketball practice to celebrate."

"Oh, yeah, of course. Just let me text my mom," I tell her. I pull out my phone and start typing a note to my mom and then decide to find a quiet corner and video chat her instead. I can't miss the look on her face when she hears the news. I inwardly squeal again.

Just as I'd guessed, Mom easily agreed to my staying after school today. She tried to hide the surprise in her voice when I told her that I'd made the cheerleading squad and she congratulated me over and over again. We all know the athletic genes in the family all went to Sophie, so who could blame her for being shocked that I actually made the squad? I've spent the whole last part of the day pinching myself.

Mackenzie waited for me by my locker while I finished loading my books into my backpack after the final bell. Colin knew something was up with me in math to put me in such a good mood and I almost told him the news. But then I thought about it again and decided he might not care about my making cheerleading or understand the significance of it. Colin and I have a good vibe going on and I generally find him easy to talk to. I sort of wanted to let him in on my secret and spill everything to him: how I was uncool at my old school and that I'd made a plan to be popular at this school and how, so far, I'm rocking the plan. But obviously I couldn't let him or anyone else at Washington in on that secret. I'll have to save all those conversations for when I talk with my old friends.

"Did Elle and them already go to the gym?" I ask Mackenzie.

"Yeah, she said just to meet her in there."

"Great." I stand and swing my backpack over one shoulder, using my free hand to smooth down my top and slam my locker shut. "Let's go."

Mackenzie and I walk into the gym and walk the perimeter so we don't interrupt the boys running drills on the court. I don't really understand basket-ball yet, except the obvious goal of making baskets. But I'm sure I'll learn quickly as we start actually cheering at games.

I scan the bleachers and see most of the girls are already sitting in the stands and talking anima-tedly. There are backpacks and coats tossed around everywhere.

"Taylor! Mackenzie!" Lola and Gianna call out when we reach them. They both get to their feet and give me a quick hug and then hug Mackenzie too.

"Isn't this awesome?" Shriya asks, joining our circle.

"We're going to have the best time," Vanessa adds, right behind.

I nod and look at each of the girls. I swallow hard. I'm feeling a little choked up. I'm really part of a group. I have friends who are truly happy I'm here. This is everything. I would seriously pinch myself if it wouldn't look weird.

"You were amazing at tryouts," I say to Vanessa. "What was that combination you did?"

"It was a running roundoff backhand back tuck. I was in gymnastics for years," she adds with a shrug. "I can teach you some day."

I have to bite my inner cheeks to keep from laughing. I was fairly sure that day would never come.

"Okay, girls," Elle calls out from behind me. We all quickly climb into the bleachers and take a seat. Elle stays standing on the gym floor, clearly ready to take charge. "I just wanted us to take some time before our first practice to get to know each other better and celebrate. This will be the best season of cheer yet, I'm sure. You guys were all amazing, and I'm so glad we're going to get to have so much fun together. So, welcome." Elle reaches down into a bag near her feet and pulls out a couple of boxes of ice cream bars. It was the same type the cafeteria sells at lunch so she must have talked one of the cafeteria ladies into giving them to her. She passes the boxes around and waits until we each have one. She unwraps hers and holds it high in the air. "Cheers to making the squad and a kick-butt season ahead! It's going to be awesome!"

"Cheers!" girls call out and some tap their ice cream bars together in a toast. It was so silly and fun and it felt special. Like, we weren't supposed to be sitting in the gym eating ice cream but, somehow, we could.

I glance over at the seventh-grade boys having

their practice and notice that a few of them are watching us and looking jealous of our ice creams.

I catch Daniel's eye and he nods at me. He gives me a thumbs-up and mouths the word, "Congrats."

Goosebumps shoot up and down my arms and I practically drop my ice cream bar. I can't believe he even noticed me or cared to pay attention to what we're doing.

And I'm not the only one who sees him. I look at Elle, and she is staring at me with a huge grin on her face.

Chapter Fourteen
TIME MARCHES ON

"It's not true, is it?" Sophie says as she barrels into my room.

"Knock much, Soph?" I set my Chromebook on the bed next to me. I've been putting the finishing touches on my parts of Elle and my online newspaper for social studies. We have to present it to the class tomorrow and then turn it in.

"Sorry, I had to find out. Are you really a cheerleader?" Sophie throws herself next to me on my bed and waits for an answer. "Like, short skirt wearing, jumping up and down and doing kicks in the air, cheerleader?"

Oh. I hadn't even thought about the uniform yet. I hope it's stylish. I look at my sister. "Yes."

"Wow! I thought for sure that Mom was pranking me. You won't even kick the soccer ball around or go jogging with Mom and me. How did you make cheerleading?"

I cross my arms and fix my gaze on her. "I just did, that's how. Geez." I'm starting to feel annoyed with her reaction.

"I'm just surprised, is all," Sophie explains. "It's so not . . . you."

"Well, maybe it's me now, okay?" I roll my eyes.

Sophie puts her hands up in surrender. "Okay, okay. You're a cheerleader. It's the new you. Good job. Did you hear I made the under-eleven indoor travel soccer team?"

I feel my anger lessen, and I smile at my sister. "No, I didn't hear. Congrats, Sophie, that's great." I know this is a big deal for her and something that she really wanted. I always knew she'd make the team, though. She's a great offensive player and scores tons of goals.

"So, we both made teams today. Seems to me like we should get ice cream for dessert. I'm going to go bug Mom and see if we've got any."

"Okay," I say and watch her leave. Ice cream twice in one day seems like a good day. I feel my phone buzzing with texts coming in and pick it up and read. The girls are texting back and forth quickly; everyone is still excited about making cheerleading today and talking about what to expect. Lola wants to know if we'll all have to wear our hair the same way. Gianna wants to know when we'll get our uniforms and what they look like. Vanessa thinks we should make color-coordinated bows. Shriya wants to know if we'll wear our uniforms to school on game days like the football cheerleaders did in the fall. I try to jump into the conversation but it's hard because it's moving so fast. I type a quick *This is going to be the most fun ever!* and then decide to switch and group text with my friends back home and tell them the news.

Taylor: Hey guys, I miss you!

Julie: Hi Taylor!!!!!!!!

Anusha: Hey girl!

Nora: Miss U 2!

Julie: How's school?

Taylor: Big news... you're not going to believe...

Anusha: ???

Taylor: I MADE THE CHEERLEADING SQUAD!! 😊😊😊

Julie: What?

Anusha: For real?!

Nora: Was it no-cut?

Taylor: 😤 Seriously, Nora? No, it wasn't no-cut. There were cuts. Just not me. I made it!

Nora: omg, congrats! That's amazing!

Anusha: Seriously, props!

Julie: I wish we could see you cheer! You have to send pics!

Taylor: I will. Believe me, I'm just as shocked as you guys are. But SO excited! And there's a boy...

Nora: Colin?

Julie: Who's Colin?

Taylor: What? No. His name is Daniel. He's on the basketball team. My friends think he likes me. I'm not sure. He congratulated me today, tho.

Anusha: Wow, you are rocking the town of Centerview and WJHS!

Julie: Seriously, we're so happy for you, Tay. You're getting everything you sought out for. Good job!

Taylor: Thanks guys!! I keep pinching myself.

I can't believe thing are really working out here.

Nora: You deserve it. ☺

Anusha: We have some news, too...

Taylor: What? SPILL!

Anusha: We're going to our first boy/girl party on Saturday night!! Like, legit. Not bowling or laser tag or anything.

Julie: It's in Audrey's basement. With music, black lights, everything!

Taylor: Wow. That sounds fantastic. Who's Audrey?

Nora: Audrey Reyes. Do you remember her?

Taylor: Hmm. Sort of. She's pretty short and wears glasses, right? I don't think I ever talked to her.

Anusha: She eats lunch with us. Her and Brittany and Katie all moved to our table and we've been hanging out some lately.

Julie: Yeah, we decided we'd try some of the tips for making friends that we were researching for you and we've branched out. It's been fun. They're super nice.

Nora: They're all in the drama club so most of the kids going to Audrey's party will be from there. We're super excited!

Julie: I still can't believe my mom is actually letting me go.

Anusha: lol, yeah, us either, J.

Nora: Haha!

Taylor: That sounds awesome! You guys will have a great time! I've got to run; my mom is calling me for dinner.

Nora: Talk soon!

Julie: Later!

Anusha: Bye!

I toss my phone on my bed and lay back on my pillows, my arms folded underneath my head. I try to figure out what exactly I'm feeling. I'm happy for my friends. I want them to have fun. But I'm feeling kind of . . . jealous? Left out? Like, why did they finally start being social and making more friends now? We never went to parties when I was still living there. And they're all able to make it to Audrey's party, a girl they've only just recently become friends with, but they couldn't find a way to make it to mine, their best friend's birthday party? I was going to have an epic boy/girl party, too, until no one showed up.

I roll over on my side and stare at the wall. I have to just let it go. I've moved and I have a new life here and they have their life there. My feelings are hurt but I remind myself that things are going pretty great here right now. I need to focus on that.

I pick up my phone and scroll through the fifty or so texts from my new friends.

Chapter Fifteen
A MINOR SLIP-UP

The cafeteria is especially noisy today as kids cram together around lunch tables and talk animatedly about their annoying teachers and favorite video games. I pull my lunch bag close to me as I carefully maneuver around a group of boys playing Keep Away with another boy's bag of M&Ms. I finally reach my table and happily slip into the last free seat between Lola and Gianna.

"Who is it?" Lola demands, looking past me at her friend.

"No one," Gianna insists. "I already told you like, a million times."

Maybe sitting between them wasn't the best idea.

"You're totally lying. Who is it?" Lola asks again.

I look back and forth between the girls, trying to decide if I should pipe in or leave this one alone. I decide to pipe in. "What's going on?"

"It's nothing. Just Lola being annoying," Gianna replies quickly.

"Are you two still carrying on?" Elle asks as she approaches the group. She sets her lunch tray on the table and moves her books off the seat she'd saved for herself before going up to buy lunch.

"I'm her best friend and she has to tell me everything. This is essential info she's holding back from me," Lola replies. She looks at me and adds, "Gianna has a crush on a boy in our science class and she won't tell me who it is."

"That's because I don't have a crush," Gianna replies, clearly irritated. "You just keep saying that I do."

Elle turns toward the far north end of the cafeteria where the stage is. Since our school doesn't have a separate auditorium, the cafeteria does double duty. I follow her gaze to where several members of the student council sit at a long table up on the stage, selling cookies. They've been doing this during lunch every day this week. Students can buy a cookie for themselves or for each other and the money is being donated to a local homeless shelter.

"Hey," Elle says, looking at Lola and then Gianna, "I'll buy you each a cookie if you stop arguing."

Both girls look like they consider this.

"Fine," Lola says. "I'll drop it for now, but you're telling me later."

Gianna's only response to Lola is to roll her eyes.

Elle stands and fishes some bills out of her pocket. "Anyone else want to go up there with me? What about you, Taylor? Want to buy a cookie for anyone special?" she asks, dragging out the word *special* and winking at me.

I'm momentarily confused. Who is she thinking I'd want to buy a cookie for?

"Maybe Daniel?" she prompts and I immediately understand.

"Oh, well, yeah that would be nice. Maybe tomorrow. I didn't bring any money with me today," I reply.

I glance at the lunch table to the right of ours and notice all of the girls looking at Elle standing. I would bet ten dollars that if they see Elle go buy a cookie, they all get up and go buy one too.

"So, you do have a crush on Daniel then, Taylor?" Lola, says, turning her attention on me.

I open my mouth to say something but then shut it again. What is she, the crush police today?

"Elle said you did but I didn't think so," she continues. "Although, you guys would really look cute together. Don't you think, Gianna?"

"Oh yeah, freaking adorable," Gianna says, probably happy to have the spotlight moved off of her. "You two with all that blonde hair. You'd be like human Barbie and Ken."

"Well," I begin and then stop. I'm not sure what to say next. I don't know if I exactly have a crush on Daniel. He seems like a nice enough boy and he is really good-looking. I'm not sure if that means I have a crush on him though. But I also want to fit in with the girls so if everyone else is talking about crushes and who they like then Daniel is as good as one as I could have.

"Okay, you guys," Elle says, "leave Taylor alone. No more teasing." She smiles at me.

I smile back, genuinely relieved for the conversation to be cut short, even if it's only a temporary reprieve.

Elle pushes her seat in close to the table. "I'll be right back."

"Wait, I'll go with you to get a cookie," Vanessa says, standing up. "My lunch is so gross, I can't eat it. My stepmom moved out so my Dad made it today. He sucks at making lunch."

Everyone turns their attention to Vanessa. Lola and Gianna give her sad eyes and Shriya frowns.

"What happened?" Lola asks.

"With my stepmom?"

Lola nods.

"I don't know. They've been fighting a lot. I think they're going to get separated. Which really sucks since she's the one who takes me shopping and to get my hair done."

The whole table is quiet and there's a heavy sense of sadness.

Elle throws an arm around Vanessa. "C'mon, I'm buying you a cookie too," she says, smiling at her friend.

I watch them walk toward the stage. That was really nice of Elle. I like it when she shows her sweet side.

Just as I'd suspected, once Elle is twenty feet away, three of the girls from the table next to us scramble to their feet and race toward the stage to buy cookies. They're probably hoping they'll get a chance to make idle chatter with her while they wait in line. I smile to myself.

Shriya drums her hands on the table to get our attention. "Okay, now that Elle is gone, I was thinking we should talk gift. I think we should get her something to congratulate her for making cheer captain. Like, a little cheerleading bear with pompoms or something. And a congratulations card that we can all sign. You guys in?"

"Yes!" Lola says.

"Definitely," I say. "It sounds perfect." And Elle would totally love it. Not to mention she did something nice for all of us at our celebration yesterday so it's a nice gesture to do something for her in return.

"Count me in," Mackenzie says. She rips open a small bag of popcorn and tosses a few kernels in her mouth.

"Me too," Gianna adds.

"Great, I'll get my mom to take me to get it and then just let you guys know how much it costs so we can split it up."

"That's a really great idea, Shriya," I say and she

beams. Out of the entire group, I've probably spoken with Shriya the least but there is one thing I can tell for sure about her: she lives to please Elle. She practically skips beside her like a faithful puppy dog throughout each school day. She watches Elle's every move like she's conducting a science lab on her. She never ever contradicts her and she agrees with every statement Elle makes. If Elle said all mechanical pencils should be banned, Shriya would start a petition. If Elle announced that she was switching her diet to only eat things that begin with the letter M, Shriya would be lugging milk, marshmallows, and macadamia nuts to school tomorrow. I can already envision Shriya's radiant smile when she gets to present the bear to Elle.

Shriya glances over her shoulder then back at us. "Quick, change the subject. They're coming back."

"Did you guys see the video Bella Bennett uploaded to her Instagram last night?" I ask. "It had something like, eleven million hits in the first hour."

"Wow, that's crazy," Gianna replies. "I didn't see it yet, but I did finally talk my mom into ordering me one of her lip kits."

"Really?" Mackenzie asks. "My mom says they're

too expensive. That and she doesn't want me wearing lipstick yet."

"Which one did you get?" Elle asks, rejoining the table. She slides a cookie toward Gianna and another toward Lola.

"Thanks," the girls say in unison.

"She bought me the pale pink one," Gianna adds, breaking a chunk off of her cookie.

"I have Autumn," Elle replies.

I nod along but don't say anything. I've never bought a Bella Bennett lip kit but maybe I should talk to Mom about it and see if she'll get me one.

"So, what are we going to do this weekend?" Elle asks. "I have to get out of my house."

"Maybe we can hang out at one of our houses?" Lola suggests. "I vote for Gianna's. She has Netflix in her bedroom."

"I can't have people over. My mom is letting me have a sleepover for my birthday in three weeks. Mark your calendars, it'll be that Saturday night. She won't let me have people over so close to that."

"Three weeks?" Shriya repeats. "That's the same night as Carrie Montgomery's birthday sleepover."

"What?" Gianna asks, a look of panic on her face.

"We can't have parties the same night. It'll make everyone have to choose whose to go to."

"Can you change yours?" Lola asks.

Gianna frowns. "I don't want to change mine. It's on my actual birthday. Carrie should change hers."

"It's Carrie's real birthday, too," Shriya says. "She's been talking about it a lot in English class. She's already told several of our friends."

"Ugh! No fair. What are the chances that we both have the exact same birthday?" Gianna moans.

"The chances are actually pretty good," I say. "Ever hear of the Birthday Paradox? In a room of twenty-three people, there is a fifty percent chance of two people having the same birthday. In a room of seventy-five people, that number goes up to a ninety-nine point nine percent chance. It's actually a simple equation," I say, excitedly. "With twenty-three people you get two hundred and fifty-three pairs. You just multiply twenty-three by twenty-two and divide by two to get that. If you're only comparing one person to another then there is only a one in three hundred and sixty-five chance they won't have the same birthday. But when you compare two hundred and fifty-three . . ."

"Are you kidding me?" Elle interrupts me abruptly, her voice harsh with annoyance.

I look at her, completely shocked.

"Enough with the math already, Taylor. It's bad enough when we have to actually endure it in class." She takes a deep breath and smiles as she looks at the other girls. "Now, what are we going to do this weekend?"

"My house is out," Vanessa says, not missing a beat.

"I can try talking to my mom," Shriya suggests.

I just sit, staring at my lunch. I had forgotten myself for a moment there. I'd been pretty careful up until this point to always present myself in a certain way when I was around this group of friends. Of course, they wouldn't want to hear about the Birthday Paradox. I can't help thinking that Colin would have liked to hear about it, though. He probably would have sat with me and worked out the chances for the whole grade and whole school too. My friends back home may not have been interested in what I was saying subject wise, but they never would have shut me down like that. They would have listened to me only because it was something I was excited about.

I can't believe Elle cut me off so rudely like that. That really stung. Okay, maybe I was off on a tangent, but she didn't have to be so mean. Oh, who am I kidding? It's not like her reaction was out of character for her. I've seen her talk like that to enough people since I've started school here. But she hadn't really spoken to me like that yet. My feelings are hurt and I'm not sure how to recover quickly from this. I know I have to figure it out fast though. I can't sit here and sulk. I need to get my head back in the game. I've come too far to give up now.

I reach up and touch my cheeks. They still feel hot from the humiliation of being silenced like that. I glance around the table. The rest of the girls are still tossing around ideas for what to do and no one is actually paying any attention to me. Except for Mackenzie. She gives me a sympathetic smile.

Mackenzie gets up and tosses out her trash and then pulls her chair over next to mine and sits down.

I appreciate the kind gesture and smile at her. I pack up my own lunch bag, unable to eat anything else, and cross my arms over my chest.

"I've got it," Elle suddenly announces loudly to the

table. She stands up and walks off toward the boys' table where Daniel is sitting with his friends.

"What do you suppose she's up to?" I whisper to Mackenzie.

Mackenzie shakes her head slowly. "Who knows?"

Chapter Sixteen
First Cheer Practice

I pull my pink Under Armour sweatshirt up over my head to reveal a cute matching pink tee-shirt underneath. I'd picked this out to wear with plain black leggings today so that I'd be comfy and ready to go quickly after school. I toss my sweatshirt onto my backpack sitting on the gym floor, against the wall, and then pull a hairband off my wrist and scoop my hair into a ponytail. I'd already refilled my water bottle before entering the gym so I'm ready to start our first day of cheer practice.

I do a quick count and there are twenty girls in the room, ten eighth graders and ten seventh graders. We'll be doing our practices together since we share the cheer sponsor, Mrs. Black, and she has to monitor both groups, but we won't be actually cheering at any of the games together. The seventh-grade basketball team generally plays the first game and the eighth graders do the second. We each cheer for our own grade.

Several of the girls are sitting on the ground stretching so I join them and follow suit. I pick a spot near Lola and Gianna, and I scan the room for Mackenzie but don't see her.

I fold forward and reach for my toes. Maybe by the time basketball season is over I'll be flexible enough to reach them.

"I'm here, I'm here," Mackenzie says from behind me. She drops all of her stuff near mine and rushes over to me. "I'm late. I couldn't get out of Art class. The teacher kept going on and on. I swear she made some people miss their busses."

"You're here now; that's all that matters," I say. "Besides, I don't think Elle or Mrs. Black even noticed."

"Good."

Elle calls us over to her to sit in a circle and she hands a stack of papers to Shriya, on her left. She explains that at each practice we'll start with warm-ups, then try to learn five to ten simple cheers, and finish with practicing kicks and jumps. By the time we have the first game, we should have a good amount or material to choose from.

I'm still feeling the sting from Elle's snapping at me during lunch today. But I know I have to get over it and move on. This is how Elle is, and if I want to stay in this group with these girls, I just have to accept it. And to be fair, I had let a side of myself show that Elle wasn't familiar with. I had let out a piece of the real me, and I'm pretty sure if Elle had met the real me on that first day of school, we never would have become friends. She probably would have been glaring at me and calling me a loser too. I'm the one trying to fit into her world, not the other way around.

I take a quick glance at the sheet of short, poem-like cheers that was just handed to me. They look super simple. Relief floods over me.

Elle guides us through a ten-minute warmup to music. I carefully watch the girls around me and mimic their movements. It feels a bit awkward since I'm not used to moving my body this way but I'm getting through it and I don't think I stand out too much.

Elle turns off the music and instructs us to grab our cheer sheets and sit in a circle.

"Take a moment to read through each cheer," she says. "First, we'll practice saying the cheers together in clear, well-projected voices. If we can't be heard, all this is pointless, right?" Her gaze roams around the circle, expectantly.

A few of the girls laugh.

"And then we'll run through the coordinated motions," she continues. "We'll work on keeping each move tight and precise. Then we'll put it all together."

I lean over slightly to whisper to Mackenzie. "This doesn't seem too hard does it?"

She looks at me and smiles and I can see she's feeling the exact same thing. "We've got this," she whispers.

Elle stops talking and gives Makenzie a look.

Mackenzie blinks at her, trying to look innocent.

I pick up my paper and pretend to be studying the words so that I don't laugh. Elle is taking her cheer captain position super seriously.

The cheers are simple and to the point. There's one where we simply say, "We are proud of you, we are proud of you." I imagine it will come across jazzier once we learn the movements and beat to the words. There's another cheer where we say, "Big G, little O, go lions, go lions, go." And then repeat. Lions are our school's mascot. There's a cheer where we say, "Hey (other team), check us out, the Washington Lions gonna rock the house." And there are several cheers that go along with things happening in the game. For example, if our player gets a free throw and he makes the basket, we say, "Whoop there it is," and make a motion like we're making a basket. If he misses the free throw, we say, "G, double O, D, T, R, Y, good try, good try, good try. Shake it off." We seem to do a lot of spelling in cheerleading.

An hour passes by quickly, and I'm feeling really good about how it's going. I don't know what I was so afraid of with cheerleading because, so far, it's a breeze. Sure, we haven't gotten to kicks and jumps yet, and maybe that will be my downfall, but I'm doing great with the movements and words. It sort of reminds me of some of the sing-song clapping games we used to play in first and second grade.

It's not the kind of activity or team I ever envisioned myself in, but so far it's been fun. I'm getting to hang out with my friends outside of school and everyone is being super nice. Especially Elle. She hasn't made fun of anyone the entire practice. She's actually been kind and encouraging to me even though I know I need the most work out of the entire group.

Elle tells us to take a break and Mackenzie and I head for our backpacks. I pull my water bottle out of the side pocket and Mackenzie pops open a sparkling water. We plop down on the ground, facing each other.

"It's pretty easy, huh?" Mackenzie says and then takes a sip.

"Yeah, it is. But I bet the hard stuff is still to come."

"Probably," she agrees.

I glance over at Elle to make sure she can't hear me and then lean in toward Mackenzie. "Can I be honest?"

Mackenzie nods and tilts back her can to drink some more.

"I don't understand some of the cheers. Like, why are we yelling directions at them? It's not like we're coaches. And don't they already know what to do? Won't we just annoy them? Are they going to rebound the ball just because I've spelled in out in a loud clear voice for them?"

Mackenzie spit laughs Le Croix onto the gym floor. Her eyes tear up and she wipes at them. "Geez, warn me next time, won't you?"

"What's so funny?" Elle says, joining us on the ground.

I don't want Elle to know I was making fun of the cheers so I have to think fast. "One of the girls keeps spelling *offense* with only one f."

"You're kidding," Elle says, sounding annoyed. She scans the room of girls sitting around on break. "Who was it, Sadie? She's always been terrible with spelling. I'll have to speak with her."

"Um, I think so," I say.

Mackenzie looks at me like she's fighting back more laughter.

I shrug and make a "whoops" face at her. I didn't mean to throw Sadie under the bus like that.

Elle cracks open her water bottle and takes a sip. "She should have had spelling nailed down by the end of first grade." She glares in Sadie's direction.

Yikes. I'm starting to feel bad that Elle is actually irritated with Sadie and not letting this go so easily. I have to diffuse the situation a bit. "She'll get it," I say brightly. "I'm sure the whole offense/defense thing gets confusing."

Mackenzie is trying so hard not to laugh that she has a vein throbbing on the side of her forehead.

Elle stands up and stretches. "Maybe. Well, back to work," she says and heads for the center of the gym.

Mackenzie falls forward, grabbing both of my knees with her hands, her shoulders shaking from silent laughing. "I thought I was going to pee my pants," she says when she straightens back up. She wipes at the tears in her eyes with the backs of her hands.

"I know, me too," I say, a giggle escaping. It feels so good to laugh with a real friend.

"Let's get going," Elle calls out to the group a few moments later.

All of the girls scramble up off of the floor, some stretching their arms over head, ready to resume practice.

"Sadie," Elle says, "can you join me up here?"

A cold shiver runs down my spine. No . . . she wouldn't. Would she?

I glace at Mackenzie and she's staring at Elle, her mouth hung open. Sadie gives the friend she'd been sitting with a questioning look and then slowly walks toward the center of the gym.

Please don't make a scene, please don't make a scene, I repeat over and over again in my mind.

Sadie takes a spot next to Elle and faces the rest of us. She smiles but she looks nervous.

Elle crosses her arms over her chest. "I want you to spell *offense* in a loud, clear voice for everyone."

Sadie looks surprised at Elle's request. "Offense?" she repeats.

Elle gives her what can only be described as a snarky head bob. "Yes. Now, please."

I want to cover my eyes with my hands, but I can't move. This is all so uncomfortable.

Sadie shrugs and then spells out *o-f-f-e-n-s-e*.

She sounded great and spelled it correctly. A feeling of relief runs through me. Good, now Elle can let this go and return to practice.

"Again," Elle says, her voice hard and cold.

Oh no. She's not going to let this go. I look at Mackenzie again, who has her head slightly turned away now and one hand over her mouth.

Elle made Sadie spell *offense* four more times before she let her return to her spot in the group. The poor girl's face was so red by that point, and I felt just horrible for her. I can't believe Elle embarrassed her like that and it was all my fault. I have to be more careful about what I say.

Chapter Seventeen
BIG NEWS

The whole school slowly crams into the cafeteria to hang out until the first bell rings every morning. As parents drop their kids off from the car lane and the buses unload at the side door, the room gets more and more packed. My friends and I are sitting in a tight circle right in the middle of the morning chaos. It feels good to have people to keep company with while we have to wait to be let into the hallways and go to our lockers. I never had anyone to wait with before first bell at my old school. Julie always had ice skating practice. Nora's bus was one of the last ones to drop off. And Anusha's mom was constantly running late. I would carry a book with me each morning and pretend like I was reading it, but I was really listening to conversations around me and wishing someone would notice me and invite me into their group.

"I was going to wait until lunch time to spill some news, but I don't think I can wait," Elle announces to us. She leans back on her hands and crosses her long legs in front of her, taking up most of the little available space we've carved out for ourselves.

"What?" Gianna asks.

"Tell us," Lola adds.

"I already know," Shriya says smugly. She looks from Elle to the rest of the group and beams because she's in the know.

"Actually, it's a bit of a surprise for Taylor," Elle says, looking straight at me.

"Me?" I ask, confused. What kind of surprise could Elle have cooked up for me? And should I be scared?

"I orchestrated a group activity for us for Friday night. We're going to meet the guys: Daniel, Braydon, Coleson, and Jacob at the cineplex for a movie."

Lola and Gianna exchange surprised looks.

"It's not going to be a DC Comic movie, is it?" Vanessa asks. "I can not watch another Batman, I just can't."

"I don't know, maybe?" Elle says. "We still need to talk about which movie to see."

"How is it a surprise for Taylor?" Mackenzie asks, getting to the point.

"Taylor and Daniel will be on a date," Elle replies, excitedly.

I look up at her, surprised. "I will?"

She looks at me like I just asked the stupidest question on earth. "Well, yeah. You guys will sit together and stuff. So, it's basically a date."

My eyebrows shoot up and I feel my jaw drop open. A date? I can't go on a date. Can I? I'm only twelve. I didn't think I'd have my first date until I was, I don't know, sixteen? At least in high school. I'm not ready to go on a date. I wouldn't know the first thing to do on a date. My parents are never going to go for this. My mind is racing and I can't string together the words to reply to Elle. I know she's waiting for me to say something, anything, but I'm grappling for the right thing to say. If I protest or say no, she and the other girls will think I'm pathetic and question why they're hanging out with me. But if I go along with it, I just don't know what I'll do.

"I organized this for you, you know," Elle says, studying my face.

Is she waiting for me to thank her?

"Daniel is the cutest boy in our grade, and you said that you liked him," she continues. "You've got to strike while being the new girl is hot."

She looks pointedly at me, waiting for my response I know, but it's like my mouth is full of peanut butter.

"Are you okay?" Elle asks. "You're making a face."

Oh geez, I am? I reach up and touch my cheek and I do feel warm. I have to get control of my emotions and fast. I wrack my brain for the right words and suddenly Nora and the day me and the girls went to the mall to work on Project Make Taylor Popular pops into my mind. Nora had said that her dad used a "fake it 'til you make it" technique so that his clients never knew if he didn't know something or if he was uncomfortable. She said people lose confidence in you if you flounder and are unsure of yourself so pretend like you know exactly what to do and then just figure it out later when those people aren't around.

Suddenly my mouth waters for the cotton candy frappe I had that day, sitting in the mall with the girls. I haven't had my favorite drink since we moved to Centerview. I'm not sure if there even is a coffee shop here with a secret menu like we had back home.

I feel a pang of homesickness and wish I was with Nora, Anusha, and Julie right now. They would never pressure me into a date with a boy I don't really know.

But I have to get my head in the game. I fix a smile on my face and try to look excited. "I'm fine," I say, a little too loudly. "And I *love* that idea, Elle. Thanks so much for looking out for me."

"You're welcome," she replies, sitting up straighter, obviously proud of the good deed that she thinks she's done. "We'll have a great time and don't worry, we'll all be there so you won't be nervous or anything. I can even give you some tips if you need."

Dating tips from Elle? I never would have expected that. "Great! It sounds super fun." I keep a smile plastered to my face as the conversation moves to what everyone will wear to the movie theater Friday night but inside I'm dying.

I've been stressing all morning about this Friday night date looming ahead. Mostly I've been wondering what Elle said to Daniel when she set this whole thing up. Did she say I thought he was so cute and just dying to go on a date with him? What must he and his friends be saying about me now? I saw him once in the hallway between third and fourth period and I swear my cheeks set fire. I was so embarrassed. How am I going to sit with him in the movie theater if I'm this nervous now? I could barely eat during lunch. I kept wondering if he was looking over at our table or if he would stop by and say something to me. Thankfully he didn't. I need more time to digest all of this before I have to talk to him face-to-face.

I'm so happy to get into math class and get away from any chance of running into Daniel or Elle or any of the other girls. Math is the only place I can relax and let my guard down.

"Hey, Taylor," Colin says.

I drop my books on our table and slip into the chair. "Hey, Colin. How's your day going?"

"Good. There's D&D club after school today."

"There is? We have D&D club here at Washington?" I'm shocked. Why haven't I heard about this before now? Probably because the friends I hang out with here don't play D&D.

"Yeah," Colin says. "It's only twice a month. I'll be there with my friends. You should come."

I study Colin's friendly face. He looks like he genuinely wants me there. And I would truly love to go. But

I know it can't happen. "I wish I could," I tell him. "But I have cheerleading practice every day after school."

He looks kind of bummed. "Oh, well, that's important, too," he says but I'm not sure he really means it. He probably can't figure out why anyone would want to jump around and yell at games and why they have to practice for it beforehand.

The old me would be thinking this exact thing.

"Sorry," I add.

He shrugs like it's no big deal.

Mr. Martinez pushes back from his desk and clears his throat, ready to start the class. We're still working on bivariate data. "Yesterday," he begins, "you worked on analyzing scatter plots and you found that while some relationships and patterns can be seen in the graph, they are not always obvious. You also learned that two variables may have a statistical relationship, but that doesn't mean they always have a causal relationship. Today, you and your partner will work on constructing and analyzing relationships in scatter plots." Mr. Martinez moves from row to row of tables, passing back stacks of graph paper.

Colin and I exchange smiles. We work really well together and both know this will be easy for us.

Mr. Martinez puts up a slide with the data we are to use for our scatter plot and I lean in toward Colin, ready to work.

"Do you have big plans for the weekend?" Coin whispers.

I open my mouth to talk but then shut it quickly. I do have plans with Elle and Daniel and everyone but I don't want Colin to know about our pseudo-date. I can't imagine what he'd think about it. I think quickly. "I do," I tell him. "Short trip back home to see my grandparents." It's a minor lie but he'll never know.

"That will be nice for you to be back home. Maybe you'll see your friends?"

I nod. "Maybe. Let's get to work," I say, changing subjects. It's bad enough I lied to him; I don't want to keep adding to it.

Chapter Eighteen
INSTA-NO!

It's the third day of cheer practice and I feel like I'm starting to get the hang of it. I'm even able to do a few of the jumps and kicks. Although, my jumps are not as high as everyone else's. I'm sure as I practice I'll get better. During warmups we've been doing repetitive right kicks and left kicks and I'm getting pretty good at those. Elle even mentioned it to me. Even though I've struggled with this whole idea of cheerleading and being a cheerleader, it did feel good to receive the compliment. And I'm having so much fun hanging out with my friends and getting the extra time to talk and laugh outside of classes and lunch. I do wish I would have been able to go to that D&D

club with Colin and his friends yesterday but there
will be other opportunities, maybe after cheer season is over.

Elle calls for a water break and I remember that I
didn't have time to refill my water bottle before practice today.

"I'm going to go refill," I say to Mackenzie, giving
my bottle a shake to explain.

"I'll come with you," she says.

We head for the door and I happen to glance at
Sadie. She has her water bottle up to her lips and I
swear she's glaring at me as she drinks. We haven't
spoken at all since Elle embarrassed her in front of
the whole group at the first practice. I think she's
somehow figured out that I'm the one who told Elle
she couldn't spell *offense*. She hasn't said anything to
me about it though, I think, because she knows Elle
and I are friends. I still do feel bad about that but I
haven't tried to talk to her because, frankly, I just
don't know what I'd say. I don't want to get into a fight.
I've just been hoping she'd forgive and forget.

I hear Elle call out, "Wait for us," just before
Mackenzie and I push through the exit. I turn and
see her, Shriya, and Vanessa all carrying their water

bottles and walking quickly toward us. I look over at Sadie again and she's now busily retying her shoe. It's just as I thought. As long as Elle is around, she's not going to say anything to me. I feel a bit of relief.

Our group heads out of the gym and down the hall to the water fountain. It's one of those fountains equipped to easily fill water bottles and it tracks how many bottles have been refilled at it. There is a digital message running along the top that displays how many plastic bottles were saved from ending up in landfill. This particular fountain was at 49,212 refills.

We talk as we take turns filling up our bottles.

"Are you so excited about tomorrow night?" Elle asks me.

"Ooooh," Vanessa says, grinning at me.

They're talking about the big "date." That's all anyone could talk about the entire lunch period today too.

I finish filling up my bottle and move to the side so Mackenzie can fill up hers. "I am," I say. "Nervous though, too," I add, being honest.

"Don't be," Elle tells me. "I know Daniel is excited."

"Is he?" I ask. I wonder how she knows this. Has

he been talking to Elle about me? Maybe he's been asking questions about me. If so, I wonder what Elle has been saying.

"Of course he is," she replies and doesn't elaborate further.

"I saw you guys talking in the hallway earlier today, too," Shirya adds.

I glance at her. She said that like it was some top-secret meeting we had and I'm trying to keep it hidden from the group.

"You were? You didn't tell me," Elle says.

"First I'm hearing about it," Vanessa adds.

I wouldn't exactly call it talking, I think. He said, "Hey, Taylor," as he strolled by my locker and I replied, "Hey, Daniel."

"It really wasn't anything," I say, kinda annoyed that Shriya is making it sound bigger than it really was. "I still can't believe my mom was okay with me going," I add, trying to change the subject.

Of course, maybe I wasn't as clear as I could be when I told her. In the car on the way home after practice last night, I told Mom that Elle and everyone was planning a big group movie thing for Friday night and I asked her if I could go. She said yes right away. And then she got a little emotional about it, which was sort of weird. She said she was happy that I was making so many friends at the new school and that this move might have been the best thing for everybody.

"Of course she's okay with the movie," Elle replies. "What would she have to worry about with all of us there?"

"My mom was a little hesitant," Mackenzie pipes in, "and I'm not the one on a 'date.' She just hasn't let me go to the movies without her or my dad yet. But I assured her there were so many of us going and all we would do is go into the movie and then get picked up so she agreed."

"Elle, Vanessa, and I went to a movie on our own before," Shriya says and Vanessa nods. The girls exchange a smug look, obviously feeling superior to those of us who haven't had this experience yet.

"We'll stick together," Elle says. "Nothing bad will happen. Unless Daniel and Taylor wander off alone somewhere," she says, teasing me.

I just raise my eyebrows at her. There is no way I'm wandering away from my friends with Daniel anywhere.

While Vanessa takes her turn filling her water bottle, I notice a couple of girls come out of the music room down the hall, violins in tow. "Oh, no," I say and nod toward the girls.

Everyone follows my gaze and Elle lets out a peel of laughter.

Shriya and Vanessa cover their mouths and giggle.

One of the orchestra girls has her skirt stuck up in her waistband. Luckily, she has some tights on under the skirt or this could really be devastating for her. It's still pretty embarrassing.

"I'm going to go tell her," I say to the group and move to leave.

Elle grabs my arm and yanks me back, spilling some of the water out of my bottle and onto the floor. "Don't you dare." she tells me.

I just look at her, confused. But not for long.

Elle whips out her phone and launches her Instagram app. She clicks near the top and the next thing I know, she's gone live.

Elle takes off down the hall after the two girls, recording and making some sort of comments into her phone. I have a hunch that they're not the nicest. Vanessa and Shriya chase after her, covering their mouths so they don't giggle too loudly and get the girls' attention.

Mackenzie and I don't budge. We exchange shocked looks and then watch as the two orchestra girls turn a corner. Elle, Vanessa, and Shriya walk back toward us, laughing and re-watching what Elle had just recorded on her phone.

I've seen Elle do and say some really not-so-nice things since we've become friends, but, I think this might be the cruelest thing I've seen her do.

"Wow," Elle says when her and the other two girls rejoin Mackenzie and me, "there are already like, five comments from other kids who go to school here. This is awesome!"

But it's not awesome at all. In fact, the whole scene is giving me a stomachache.

Chapter Nineteen
The Date

Mackenzie and I are sitting in the back seat of my parents' family car, heading for the Cinemark in the next town. My mom is driving us to the theater and Mackenzie's dad is picking us up once the movie is over. I'm so glad our parents agreed to this arrangement because there was no way I was walking into the movie tonight alone. Mom had to walk up to Mackenzie's door and officially meet her parents, of course, before she would feel good about another parent picking me up. And she's asked me at least a half a dozen times now if I have my phone for emergencies and money for popcorn. She actually wanted me to practice what I would say to order my popcorn and small soda at the concession stand. I wouldn't do it though. How embarrassing. She acts like I'm still a baby sometimes.

Elle had sent a mass text to all the girls and boys going on the outing, telling us to meet in the small arcade in the front of the theater's lobby at 6:45 p.m. Our movie actually starts at 7:30 p.m. so we're going to goof around with the games for a while before hand.

It took me forever to put together the right outfit to wear for our "date" tonight. I tried texting Nora, Julie, and Anusha for advice but they were all busy. All I got back was a quick text from Nora that said, *We're in the theater getting ready to watch Audrey's drama club's play. Gotta turn phone off now.* And that was it. I guess my old friends are too busy for me now that they've found new friends to hang out with. I didn't want to text Elle before the movie because I felt like she might make me more nervous than I already am. So, I took a pic of myself in my bathroom mirror and sent it to Mackenzie. She replied right away that my light gray varsity striped sleeve crop tee with mint green jeans and gray converse shoes was the perfect choice.

Mom pulls up next to the concrete stairs that

lead up into the theater. The Cinemark sign is red and enormous across the front of the giant building and the white lights running all along the ceiling near the three large ticket booths are glowing through the front glass windows. There is a small, one-room theater in Centerview called the Rialto. Mom and Dad took Sophie and me to it once since we've moved here. It has an old-fashioned marque in front under the sign where they push in plastic letters, spelling out the movie and show times each week, and only one glass ticket booth is setup outside where a guy in a red vest and black bowtie sits selling tickets. The inside is kind of old looking with dark red velvet seats and heavy velvet curtains that drape each side of the movie screen. They only change the movie every few weeks and the selections are usually older movies so Elle didn't want us to go there for our big group outing. The Cinemark is much bigger and busier on a Friday night. Groups of teens and families flood in to see one of the twelve movies playing and lines to the registers at the concession stands are at least ten people deep. The smell of the buttery popcorn is both overwhelming and alluring.

I open the car door, slip out of my seat, and step onto the pavement, waiting for Mackenzie to join me. My stomach is doing major flips.

Mom looks nervous, too, her eyes darting from the doors to the theater and back to me. "You're sure you have your phone? And money?"

I nod, fighting off the urge to talk Mom into coming in with us just to buy the tickets.

"We'll be fine, Mrs. Hunt," Mackenzie says. "I have my phone too. And I've gone to the movies with friends before. Taylor and I will stick together."

I shoot Mackenzie a grateful look. I know that isn't totally true since we just had been talking about this exact scenario earlier. Mackenzie and I haven't been friends for that long but she seems to get me. She senses my nervousness and instead of making fun of me like Elle would, she reassures me.

"Okay," Mom says and then lets out a sigh. "I'm going to sit here for a minute though until I see you buy your ticket and go in."

"Okay. See ya," I say, shutting the car door.

Mackenzie and I run up the steps and into the theater. I follow her to one of the glass booths and listen as she asks for one ticket to *Space Storm III*. When she's done, I do the same and hand over the eight dollars and collect my ticket.

We head into the lobby of the theater and I see our group of friends right away. The butterflies in my stomach are whipping around like they're riding the teacups at Disney World but I do my best to try and look cool and calm as we make our way toward the group.

"Taylor! Mackenzie!" Elle says and gives us each a quick hug.

The other girls each give us hello hugs as well, even though we just saw everyone only a few hours ago at school. It's a whole different energized vibe getting to hang out on our own outside of school.

I look up at Daniel, standing with two of his friends, his hands shoved into his jean pockets. "Hey, Taylor," he says.

"Hey, Daniel," I reply. I step next to him and, unsure as to what to do with my own hands, clasp them together in front of me.

We stand there, awkwardly, for a few moments while nobody talks. I can feel my friends all staring at me and my face getting hot. I rack my brain for something to say to him, anything. But I don't really know much about Daniel other than he plays basketball and he likes candy. His blonde hair is hanging in his eyes and he shakes his head, knocking it out of his eyesight. My gaze moves down to his outfit, a tee-shirt and jeans.

"Cool shirt," I say.

He looks surprised. "You know it?"

"*Fallout 4*, right?" I ask.

He grins. "Yeah. Do you play it?"

"No, not really, but I've seen people play it," I reply. Actually, my dad plays it at home on the weekends some times. I've sat with him and watched him play before but I haven't ever played it myself.

"Cool." He looks over at the arcade and then back at me. He rocks back and forth from his heels to his toes, seeming antsy.

We're both silent and I'm trying to think of anything else at all interesting to say. Maybe I should have prepped for this at home. I could have put a list of conversation topics on my phone and snuck peeks at it. I can feel my friends still watching me, waiting for some kind of grand show from us, but I've got nothing. Daniel and I are basically strangers. This is so incredibly awkward. I can feel my mouth getting dry, and I desperately want a soda.

I wish Elle would pipe in and say something to take the pressure off me. Or what about Shriya? She's always talking. Can't she think of a funny story to share right about now?

"Let's play," Daniel's friend Braydon says, finally breaking the awful silence. He bumps Daniel in the shoulder with his own. Clearly, he's over watching our nonexistent conversation.

Daniel raises his eyebrows at me and I smile, indicating I'm fine with him going.

The girls and I watch Daniel, Braydon, and their other friend, Coleson, join Jacob, who is already on a game in the arcade.

Soon as the boys are out of earshot, Elle moves in closer and says, "He's so totally into you!"

Mackenzie gives my arm a squeeze and Vanessa and Shriya bob their heads up and down in unison, agreeing with Elle.

I shrug, not sure of what to say. I can't tell if he likes me or not. He's been pretty friendly so far but that could just be his personality.

The girls and I stand around talking while we wait for Lola and Gianna to arrive. About five minutes pass and then Elle nudges me in the shoulder and indicates with her eyes that I should look into the arcade.

Daniel looks at me and then back at the game then back at me again, like he's just remembering this is supposed to be a "date." He says something to his friends and then walks over to our group and stops in front of me.

"Want to play *Transformers Human Alliance*? We can do two-player."

"Sure," I say and follow him over to the game.

I can feel the girls all watching us as we stand in front of the game and he puts the tokens into the coin slot. I must admit, I feel a thrill that he's pulled me away from the group like this, in front of everyone. We're alone in a sense but not alone at the same time. And we have something to do so I don't have to stress about coming up with something witty to say. I wonder if any of my friends are jealous. I wonder if other kids hanging out in the arcade see us together and think that we're a couple.

After Daniel makes some selections on the screen, he picks up one of the blasters and starts shooting decepticons. Or, maybe they're autoboots, I can't be sure. I pick up my blaster and start shooting at them, too. It's actually a lot of fun. Soon we're laughing and Daniel is guiding me, telling me to turn left or watch my back.

When the game is over we rejoin the rest of the group. Lola and Gianna are here now and we're ready to hit the concessions before the movie. Everyone is chatting and cracking jokes while we wait in line for our snacks. There's an electric buzz in the air and I'm not sure about anyone else, but I'm not really feeling nervous anymore. I'm feeling excited and grownup. I'm actually out at the theater with a big group of friends and no adults.

"One small popcorn and a small orange soda, please," I tell the boy behind the concession stand.

He's tall and skinny and has pimples across his chin. I watch him punch my order into the cash register and then I hand him some money.

When we're all sufficiently snacked up, we head into the theater. We're walking down the red carpeted aisle and the group files into two rows. I follow Mackenzie into a row and then remember that I'm supposed to be sitting with Daniel. I look over my shoulder to see where he is and he's standing right behind me. I take my seat and set my drink in the cup holder and my popcorn on my lap. I'm careful not to put my arm on the armrest because I don't want to be one of those people who claims the arm rest as soon as they sit down.

The movie begins and our group quiets down to concentrate on the screen. I didn't see the first two *Space Storms* but this one is pretty good. Daniel and I don't talk during the film but we laugh and gasp at all the same parts.

When the movie ends, our entire group files out into the lobby. The guys are talking animatedly about the big battle scene at the end.

"Bathroom break girls," Elle says over the loud voices. We girls all head in the direction of the ladies' room. The boys head back to the arcade to hang out until their parents arrive to pick them up.

Once we're safely inside the bathroom, Elle flips around to face me. "Well? How was it?"

I think about what to say. It was a good first date, I guess. I'm still not sure how I feel about Daniel. He's nice and certainly cute. I liked the attention he gave me. And I liked the attention from my friends, rooting me on. It was sweet that Daniel asked me to play a video game with him; and, in the theater, he shared his M&Ms with me. But I'm not sure there is much more beyond being friends. I didn't feel my heart beat faster or my palms sweat, like I'd read happens. I felt just fine.

"It was good," I tell Elle. "He's nice."

"Isn't he? He's perfect for you," she replies. "You should make another date with him."

"Oh, uh," I stammer, "I don't know about that." I walk over to the row of sinks and wash my hands under one of the faucets, busying myself.

Elle follows close behind me. "Why not? You two are so perfect together. If you and Daniel are a couple, everyone will know who you are and be jealous. You guys will be like, the cutest couple in seventh grade."

I grab a couple of paper towels from the dispenser and dry my hands. Everyone knowing who I am is appealing, but still. I toss the paper out and turn around. All of the girls are watching me, waiting for my response.

"I'm not sure, Elle," I say. "I think this was good enough. We don't have to push it."

She raises both of her eyebrows. "You have to, Taylor. You'll regret it if you don't," she insists.

I bite my bottom lip, not sure how else to reply. She's making me uncomfortable.

"You didn't. Leave her alone, Elle," Mackenzie says. She gives Elle a look and some kind of understanding passes between them.

Shriya and Vanessa glare at Mackenzie. Lola and Gianna look like they want to disappear.

"What?" Mackenzie says. "Elle didn't want to date him anymore, so why does Taylor have to if she doesn't want to?"

My mouth drops open. Wait a minute. What's this? I look at Elle. "You dated Daniel?"

Elle throws a glare Mackenzie's way, too. She turns back to me and smiles. "We didn't really date. Not for long anyway. Just a week and a half at the start of the school year. It's ancient history."

I'm completely blown away. I can't believe they actually dated. I can't even really picture them together. It makes no sense. "If you dated him, why are you pushing so hard for me to date him?"

"Because Elle likes an eighth grader on the wrestling team. Jackson Stone," Lola explains. "He's really hot."

"She thinks it will look bad if she moves on and Daniel hasn't," Gianna adds.

I look from one friend to the next. So, everyone knows about Elle and Daniel? Doh! Well, of course they do. They've been in school together all year. Now, I feel kinda silly.

"None of that even matters, Taylor. You like him, and he likes you. That's all that counts," Elle says.

My mind is racing. This is all too weird. I have to get out of this situation. "I couldn't date your ex-boyfriend, Elle. It would be awkward," I explain.

"No, it wouldn't," she insists, shaking her head. "We've both moved on. And I'm just happy that if I'm not going to be with Daniel, then he can be with a good friend of mine." She smiles sweetly at me, like she really means what she's saying.

I stare at Elle. She thinks we're good friends? Really? Now I'm really confused. I feel like she purposely withheld information from me, basically duping me into this "date" with Daniel. I'd never have agreed to come tonight if I'd known he was her ex. But at the same time, I'm sort of honored that she already feels that I'm a good friend of hers. I need more time to sort this all out.

"I don't know," I say.

Mackenzie's phone buzzes and she looks down at it. "My dad is here. We've gotta go," she tells me.

"Okay," I say and follow her toward the bathroom exit. "See you at school, guys," I say to the girls. I wave one hand in the air as I leave.

"Don't forget to say goodbye to Daniel on the way out," Elle calls after me.

I don't reply.

Chapter Twenty
POST-DATE RECAP

"Can you pause the show while I go grab a soda?" Sophie asks me. She gets up from the couch and takes a few steps before pausing to look back at me. "You want one?"

I nod yes and hit pause on *Fuller House*. "Can you pop another bag of microwave popcorn too?"

"Sure," she replies.

Sophie and I have been binge-watching episodes on Netflix for the past two hours while Mom is out grocery shopping and Dad is upstairs doing some work. I'm still recovering from last night's "date."

The girls have been texting me off and on today, wanting to rehash different parts of the evening. But

I'm still feeling funny about the whole thing. And funny that I let myself get wrapped up in it. I never really said that I even liked Daniel, yet I let them push us into the whole "date" thing. Elle used me to get Daniel out of the way for her to make a claim on Jackson. And her reasoning didn't even make sense. Who cares if she likes a new guy? Why does Daniel have to move on for her to move on? I mull this over for a few minutes and then a possible answer comes to me. Because Elle is overly conscious of what everyone thinks of her. That's got to be it. She wouldn't be the most popular girl in the class if she wasn't constantly analyzing what people thought of her. I guess it's kind of like what I've been doing in a way.

My phone buzzes on the coffee table with an incoming text. I don't move at first, guessing it's one of the girls from school wanting to chat again about last night and how "super great" it was. And I swear, I have talked that subject to death. *Maybe it's Nora?* I think, eagerly. My excitement immediately switches to feeling let down. No, it probably won't be any of my friends from back home. They should be at the big boy/girl party at their new friend Audrey's house right about now. I'm not going to lie; my feelings are pretty hurt. My old friends were all in with me on this popularity experiment. They've been really supportive and wonderful from the start. And they knew last night was a big deal for me. But in the last two days, when I've really needed them, they've kinda let me down. I texted them all first thing this morning that I *had* to talk to them asap about everything that happened at the theater last night. But nobody replied. I guess that old saying about being out of sight and out of mind is true. They must not care about me anymore.

My phone buzzes again and curiosity gets the better of me so I reach over and pick it up.

    Are you being stuffed with cookies and
    butterscotch candies?

It's from Colin. What on Earth is he talking about? And then it dawns on me and I smile at my phone. I forgot I told him I was going to be hanging out at my grandma's house. He's never met my grandma. She's not your typical elderly woman. My grandma would be drinking margaritas and doing a salsa right about now. She always says Saturday nights are for dancing. I don't want to keep up the lie with him so I have to think of something to say.

```
I'm back home now. Kinda bored, just
hanging with my sister watching Netflix.
You?
```

The smell of popcorn hits my nose before I look up and see Sophie come back into the room. She sits on the opposite end of the couch and puts the bowl between us. "Ready to start?"

"Just a sec," I say, waiting for Colin's next text.

```
Same here. Fuller House with my sister.
```

I almost laugh out loud at the visual of Colin watching Fuller House right now too. I type fast.

```
No way, me too!
Yeah, right.
```

I take a picture or the television screen and send it to him.

He replies quickly.

```
So, we're both having exciting Saturday nights
then?
```

Just then another text comes in but in the group chat with my new friends. It's from Elle. My stomach immediately tightens and the fun, relaxing vibe

I just had going while chatting with Colin vanishes. I click over to Elle's text and read.

```
Keep next Saturday clear girls, I just
confirmed with the guys that we'll meet up
with them at the winter carnival.
```

I grimace. I've heard a little bit about the winter carnival around school. The eighth graders hold it in the school gym to raise money for their big eighth grade boat trip at the end of the school year. They take a bus to Chicago and then spend the day on a big, beautiful boat that cruises around Lake Michigan. Everyone dresses up in suits and fancy dresses and a professional photographer takes their pictures. A DJ plays music and everyone dances and has a great gourmet meal, from what I've heard. I'm not opposed to going to the carnival to support the fundraiser; after all, we'll be eighth graders next year and raising money for our own big boat trip. But I can't help wondering what Elle might be up to this time. Is she going to force me into another "date" with Daniel?

"Who was that?" Sophie asks, interrupting my thoughts. "You were grinning pretty big one minute and then your eyebrows scrunched up and you were frowning the next."

My eyes flick between Sophie and my phone. I sigh and put it down on the end table. "It's just . . . junior high stuff," I say with a shrug.

"What kind of junior high stuff?" she asks.

I bite my bottom lip and look at her, considering how much to say. "I'm not sure you'll understand."

"I understand a lot more than you think, Tay." She crosses her arms over her chest, defensively.

I sigh again. I need to talk to someone about all of this stuff and it's not like I have anybody else to talk to right now. "Well . . . okay." I turn on the couch to face Sophie and pull my knees to my chest, wrapping my arms around my legs. "I've made a lot of friends at school since we've moved to Centerview. These friends are all pretty popular so I'd guess you'd say I'm in the popular group at this school now."

"Wow," Sophie says. "That's different."

"Yeah, no kidding." I grin at her. Being in seventh grade here is worlds away from how seventh grade was back home for me. And Sophie had a front row seat to how that was at my birthday party. "Anyway, things are going really well and I don't want to mess anything up. But . . . " I pause.

Sophie blinks at me. "But what?"

"The main girl, or, kind of like, leader of the group, this girl Elle, well, she's not really all that nice. She's actually pretty mean sometimes to people not in the group. Like my friend Colin from math class. She hates him and calls him names and stuff. But I like him. He's really nice. And funny."

"Huh," Sophie says, looking like she's mulling it over.

"And you know that group friend outing to the movies last night?" I ask her. "Elle tricked me into going on a sort of 'date' with this boy Daniel to get him off her back. I didn't really want to do it but she forced me into it. I'm just sort of confused right now, and I don't know what to do," I add. "I don't like Elle's behavior but I like being in the popular group."

Sophie nods like she understands what I'm saying.

I can't believe I'm about to ask advice from my ten-year-old sister who is still in elementary school but here goes. "So, what do you think?"

Sophie clears her throat. "Well, I don't play with mean people. I say dump Elle and hang out with the kids who are nice."

I frown. That's easy for a fifth grader to say but junior high is a whole different world. I can't just dump the most popular girl in our class or I'll be right back to where I was before we moved here. I'll be sitting alone again at my next birthday party. I just can't turn back. It's not an option.

I shake my head slowly. "I don't think I can do that, Soph. I might get kicked out of the group, and I don't want to have no friends at school."

Sophie considers this. "When I have a friend that I like who is acting like a jerk," she says, "I tell her to knock it off. Like, do you remember my friend Kara at my old school?"

I nod.

"When she was teasing Samantha for having to eat a snack during class because of her diabetes, I told her she was being mean and to knock it off. She said she was sorry and we stayed friends."

I try to mentally picture myself telling Elle she is being mean and to knock it off. In my mind, it doesn't end well for me. I raise my eyebrows while I think. "I'm just not sure," I finally say.

"Well, can we turn *Fuller House* back on while you think?" Sophie asks.

"Sure," I say with a nod, knowing this wasn't the kind of problem I could just solve in one night.

I wake up Sunday morning with the corduroy pattern from our family room couch imprinted on my cheek. Sophie and I had an impromptu sleepover last night when we both fell asleep on the couch.

I sit up and stretch my arms over head, yawning. I look over and see Sophie is still sound asleep and the TV is still on, though on the general Netflix screen now. I inhale deeply and smell bacon in the air. Dad must be up and cooking breakfast in the kitchen already. He always makes a big breakfast on Sunday mornings.

I stand up and pull my cozy velour blanket off the couch and wrap it around my shoulders to bring upstairs with me. I might as well go up to my room and do a little homework until Dad says the food is ready.

I set up my homework space on my bed and then remember to check my phone. I had turned it on silent last night before going to sleep. There are like, twenty messages waiting for me.

Nora: Taylor!! Tell us everything! How was your date?

Julie: What did you wear? Did he try to kiss you?

Anusha: We have been literally dying waiting to hear from you. The cell service went out all over town yesterday!

Nora: There was a terrible storm and like a satellite was knocked out or something.

Julie: It wasn't a satellite, Nora. It was a cell tower. 😉

Anusha: TELL US ABOUT YOUR DATE!!!!!!!!!!!!!!

I smile down at my phone. My friends do care about me. They weren't ignoring me at all. I feel relieved and sad all at the same time. I'm happy that my old friends are still my true friends but I'm also sort of sad that my new friends aren't quite the same. Except for Mackenzie, of course. I feel like she and I could really become great friends. But the other girls? I don't know. I guess I thought having all these friends would feel a lot different. Then again, maybe I'm just overthinking things.

I settle back on my pillow and start typing a reply to my friends.

Taylor: First, tell me about the party! Do NOT leave out details.

Chapter Twenty-One
FIRST GAME

It's our first basketball game of the season and I'm super excited. We're decked out in the school colors and all wearing matching maroon and gold cheer tops over maroon body suits and short maroon pleated skirts with a double gold strip running around the bottom. We also have on coordinating maroon spandex shorts underneath. Elle had decided we should all wear our hair in high pony tails for the games and a few of the girls made maroon and gold ribbons for us to wear in our hair. Everybody looks great.

My parents tried to get me to play on a soccer team when I was little but I wouldn't do it. They brought me to several practices but I always refused to get up off the ground and participate. I would sit right down in the middle of the soccer field and look for four-leaf clovers in the grass while all of the other kids ran around me trying to kick the ball. They never signed me up for another sport after that. And I never felt like I was missing anything. But standing here in the gym, in coordinated outfits with the rest of the girls, it feels kind of cool to be part of a team. Even if I'm not the best at it.

"I'm nervous," Mackenzie whispers to me. Her light brown hair has extra fullness and bounce today. She must have curled it just for the game.

"Me, too," I whisper back. "I hope I can remember all of these cheers. At least we're not in the front row."

Elle had decided that we cheerleaders would stand in two staggered rows of five, just behind the hoop on the south side of the court, near the boys' locker room. The bleachers are to our left and the two basketball teams, our home team and the away team from Jefferson Junior High, are sitting on benches to our right, listening to last-minute advice from their coaches. Elle and a few of the other girls, who are really good, are standing in the front. Mackenzie and I both volunteered to go in the back. I feel pretty confident with the cheers we've prepared for today, but it's still my first game so I'd rather not be front and center.

We stand in ready position, our feet spaced apart about a foot and a half with our toes slightly pointed out to the sides like a V, and our hands behind us and placed on the small of our backs, our index fingers and thumbs touching. We're supposed to stay in this position whenever we're in-between cheers. Elle has a list of all the cheers we've learned taped up to the gym wall behind us and will pick out which cheer is appropriate to do at which time. There are certain cheers that coordinate with certain parts of the game, and I'm just glad that Elle is in charge of what we're doing in terms of order because I would never know which cheer is the right one to do at which time. I'm just hoping I can follow along quick enough that I don't stand out from the rest of the girls.

One of the two black-and-white stripe-shirted referees blows his whistle and the game begins.

"Here we go!" I whisper loudly to Mackenzie.

One boy from each team stands facing each other and the referee throws the ball in the air. Both boys jump and reach for the basketball but our guy slaps it backward to one of his teammates. The crowd is cheering and stamping their feet in the stands.

"All right, girls," Elle says, "let's do Big G, Little O."

Our whole group launches into the cheer with coordinated claps, air punches, and kicks. We've practiced this one a bunch and I think we sound and look really good. When it's over, I practically want to pinch myself. I'm actually cheering at a real live game!

As I look over at the crowd filling the bleachers, I can't help but think I've made it. I worked hard to get in the popular crowd and I'm here. This must be like what those kids who spend years singing in their rooms and then finally make it onto the stage on those singing television shows feels like. But probably on a less grand level. There are large clusters of students from all three grades in the school here to watch the game. I'm guessing some of them may even be jealous of us and wishing they were in our spots. It wasn't that long ago that I was in their place, wishing I was friends with the popular girls. I think being on both sides of the gym really allows me to appreciate my current position. It feels good, and I don't want to forget it.

The gym is loud with parents cheering on their sons, coaches jumping out of their seats every two minutes to yell out plays, and referees blowing their whistles. The booming of the boys' pounding feet as they run up and down the court is so strong I think I can feel the vibration in my own feet as I stand here. Add to it the buzzer going off from the scoreboard overhead every so often and the smell of sweaty boys as they rebound a ball only two feet from where I'm standing and my senses are near overload. There is so much going on around me that my head is practically spinning. Yet it's still feeling fun to me.

"All right, girls," Elle calls. "Next up, Rock the House."

We swoosh our hips and skirts side to side in beat to the cheer, jumping and high kicking in all the right spots. My high kick isn't nearly as high as the other girls' but it's not terrible either. We have to yell really loud to be heard over the excited crowd. I'm guessing my throat will be sore tomorrow.

"Nice kick, sweetheart!" a man from the bleachers yells. He shakes a gold pompom in the air and smiles at us.

The man next to him is holding a sign with maroon

and gold glitter lettering. It says, "Cheer Hard, E.B.!" and there are smaller phrases surrounding the edges of the sign like, "Go, fight, win!" and "You got this!"

"Your timing is perfect, babe!" he calls out.

I give them a puzzled look and lean in toward Mackenzie. "Who are those guys?" I nod my head toward the men in the bleachers.

Mackenzie looks to where I nodded and smiles. "Oh, those are Elle's dads. They met while competing at the national cheerleading finals in college or something so they're super into cheer."

"So, E.B.?"

"Elles Belles," Mackenzie says. "That's their nickname for her. Only child," she adds with a grin.

"Ah, got it. And they come to cheer for the cheerleader. I like it," I say with an approving nod.

Elle tosses a look at Mackenzie and me and we immediately know we should hush. We both place our hands behind our backs in ready stance for the next cheer. It's so loud in the gym that I don't think anyone could have even heard our conversation anyway but I get that we should be ready to cheer at all times.

"All right, guys," Elle says, checking the cheer sheet taped to the gym wall behind us again. "Victory."

"You can see why Elle is so serious about cheer-leading," Mackenzie whispers. "It's genetic."

"Totally."

One of the coaches calls a time out and the teams sub in new players. Daniel jogs out to the middle of the court. He grins and waves at me as he gets into position. I can literally feel my cheeks burning. Did anyone else see that? I glance at Elle who has her head turned toward me and is giving me a smug look. Vanessa give me a thumb's up. I guess my question is answered. They totally saw.

The game restarts and Daniel looks like he's pretty good as far I can tell. He charges back and forth down the court with the rest of the guys and makes a basket from pretty far away.

There is a minor commotion going on at the other end of the gym where the booster parents sit and sell candy. I'm distracted watching another mom with her young son's shoulder clutched in one hand while the other hand shakes a box of candy at the booster par-ents. I can't be a hundred percent sure what's going on but from trying to read her lips, I think she's say-ing something about nuts. Maybe her son is allergic to nuts and it's in the candy he bought?

In a flash, Daniel's hand flies in front of my face, batting a basketball, and I stumble backward.

"Oh em gee," Gianna says dramatically, "he like, totally saved your life."

"I think that is the most romantic thing I've ever seen in real life," Lola says.

"So brave," Vanessa adds.

Elle just smiles at me with her I-told-you-so look fixed firmly on her face.

"Okay," I say, trying to laugh a little, "it wasn't that serious."

"You almost did get clocked right in the side of your head by the ball. What were you looking at?" Mackenzie asks.

I glance over at the candy stand again but that parent is gone now. "Nothing," I say. My eyes wander over the court until I find Daniel.

He puts a thumb up and raises his eyebrows, questioning if I'm okay.

I nod and smile, feeling a bit overwhelmed by it all.

"You okay, Taylor?" Elle asks, interrupting my thoughts.

"I'm fine," I say.

"All right then," she says louder and to all of the girls. "Ready with the free throw cheers."

We all stand in superman pose and wait for the fouled-on boy to shoot at the basket.

Chapter Twenty-Two
COUPLED UP

I think Daniel and I are a thing. He never asked me to be a thing with him and I never agreed to be a thing with him but everyone is acting like we're a thing so I guess we're just a thing now. And . . . I'm slightly freaking out.

It feels all a little "medieval times" to me, to tell the truth. Boy stops basketball from pummeling girl in the face and girl is now betrothed to him. Okay, it may not be as serious as all that, but a shift has definitely taken place and everyone knows it. It's lunch time and Daniel and his friends are squished into our already too tight lunch table with Daniel sitting wedged in right next to me. I can literally smell the garlic from the slice of pizza he ate on his breath. And he keeps helping himself to my baby carrots. It's just plain weird.

It doesn't help that I can see Lola and Gianna giggling and talking about me across the table. It's kind of obnoxious, and I'm pretending like I don't hear them but it's getting harder by the minute. At least Mackenzie is squished in on my other side and passing me a commiserating glance here and there. It seems like she's the only one who actually knows how I feel. She pulls out one of her Oreos from a small Ziploc bag and slides it over to me on a napkin. I smile my thanks.

Daniel is talking loudly across the table to Braydon and Coleson, who are sitting between Shriya and Vanessa, about the game last night. We ended up winning fifty-two to thirty-three. Daniel got four of the baskets. They're using a lot of basketball lingo and I'm not paying close attention to what they're saying. I am, however, studying the florescent orange macaroni sauce on Coleson's lips and teeth and wondering how long it will take him to actually notice it and wipe it off. I see Lola studying him, too, but in more of a moony kind of way, and I wonder if she's developing a crush on him.

"So, who all is definitely going to the winter carnival on Saturday?" Vanessa asks. She opens a package of Pocky sticks and slips one into her mouth.

"We're going," Daniel replies, plucking another baby carrot out of my plastic bag.

I side-eye him. Who is *we*? He can't possibly be talking about me, can he? Daniel is nice and I'm glad I'm not walking around with a giant bruise on the side of my face today, but surely he wouldn't just answer for me like that. He must be talking about him and the guys.

"I still have to check with my parents," I say firmly. There. That should let him know that only I, and well, my parents, decide where I'm going on the weekends.

"You have to go, Taylor," Elle insists. "Didn't you read my texts? I'm having a pre-carnival get-together for the girls at my house." She widens her eyes and a tiny wrinkle appears between her eyebrows, like she's truly worried I might not attend her event.

I did see a text go by saying something about the early get-together. But I didn't know it was officially on. It's just a school winter carnival and not like a formal dance we need to get dressed up for. But Elle is an organizer and likes to have things a certain way so it'd figure she wants to know what every-one is wearing beforehand and coordinate a group entry.

"What is the winter carnival like, anyway?" I ask.

"Oh, it's so much fun!" Lola says. "There are all kinds of winter-y decorations and games and lots of carnival foods like popcorn, pizza, and hot dogs. And cotton candy, of course," she adds. "The eighth graders run the games, sell the food, everything. It's a chance to hang out with kids you don't get to see all the time in school. Especially the cute boys." Lola looks at Elle and wiggles her eyebrows.

Elle pretends like she doesn't see her.

Lola must be talking about that eighth grader, Jackson Stone, that she told us about at the movie. I'm just glad it isn't me being teased for liking a boy for once.

"You have to come," Daniel says and smiles at me.

I can't help but smile back. While I might not have feelings for Daniel, it does feel nice that he wants me there. He seems like he's a pretty good guy. "Okay," I say. "I'll talk to my parents about it after school today."

"Then it's all set. We'll meet you guys at the carnival at two p.m. and the girls will all come over to my house at noon." Elle turns toward me. "I live really close to school. We can just walk from my house."

I nod. "Okay. Sounds like a plan."

I slide into my seat just before the eighth-hour second bell rings. "Close one," I whisper to Colin. I would have gotten to math earlier if Elle and Shriya hadn't cornered me in the hallway. Elle wanted to know if I had any blue or white tops. She thinks all of us girls should coordinate our outfits in wintery colors like blue, white, and silver for the carnival. But she's the only one allowed to come in silver. She said one of her dads had just ordered her the cutest cut out shoulder silver top that is perfect for the carnival. I told her I had a navy cardigan I could wear over a white tee shirt and that my sister had a pair of snowflake earrings I was sure I could borrow. Then Shriya was super annoying and said loudly to me, "A date two weekends in a row with Daniel, are you just dying?" I'd felt panic shoot straight through me for one, that Shriya was broadcasting my business, and two, that Colin might have overheard her and found out I'd lied about going to my grandma's. Luckily, he hadn't heard. But still, Shriya and her big mouth are getting on my nerves.

"For our final review of scatter plots," Mr. Martinez begins, "we'll do a class-wide project. Each of you will receive a shoe to color," he holds up a paper shoe, "and a basket of color pencils. Once you've finished designing and coloring your shoe, in pairs, I'd like you to create a quick sketch of a scatter plot using you and your partner's shoe size in men's sizes and your height in inches. If you don't know how to convert your shoe size to men's or your height to inches, jump on your Chromebooks and look it up."

I look at Colin and he shrugs.

"You'll need to determine your independent and dependent variables as well as their quantities, and then plot them on your sketch. When you're finished," Mr. Martinez says, "you'll come up and plot your points by placing your paper shoes on the large graph I made on the wall for the classroom." He points to the side of the room and, sure enough, he's made an enormous graph with black duct tape that takes up most of the wall. "When we're done," he continues, "we'll analyze the graph and then review all of the terms we've learned. And if there's still time after that, we'll begin writing the equations for the lines."

Mr. Martinez walks over to his desk and takes a seat in his chair. There's a buzz in the room as students talk to each other and set to work on their shoes.

I look at my paper and frown. It's a gym shoe. I would have loved a cute boot to decorate. Oh well, I can still make it look good. I decide I'll design my shoe to look like my favorite pink converse. Only I'll add some tiny red hearts on the side.

I study Colin as he colors his shoe orange and green with blue lightning bolts, and I try to decide if he's the type to go to a school-sponsored event outside of the school day. I'm guessing no, but it doesn't hurt to ask.

"So," I start, "I've been hearing a lot about this big winter carnival this weekend here at school."

He stops coloring and looks up. "Yeah?"

"Have you gone to it before?"

He shakes his head no.

"Oh." I pause. I keep my eyes on my shoe, scribbling the pink crayon up and down in even lines.

"Well, are you going to this one?" I stop coloring and glance at him.

He looks like he's thinking. He stops coloring too and looks over at me. "I don't know. Are you going?"

"Yeah," I reply. "I'll be there. My friends are all telling me I have to go."

"Maybe I'll go then, too," he says with a smile.

Whoa. What was that feeling? My stomach totally did one of those flippy things. There's a warmth in my chest and I'm feeling tingly, like, a little goosebumpy or something. Oh wow, do I like Colin? No . . . it's impossible. He's my friend, my buddy. But I am feeling some kind of way and it's more than how I feel when I'm with Daniel. Yikes, I think I'm blushing. I can feel my cheeks getting warm. And Colin is still smiling at me so he probably totally noticed. Gah!

"Great," I reply quickly, furiously coloring again.

"I'll talk it over with my friends and see if they want to go."

"Cool," I say, trying to sound nonchalant about the whole thing. Which is just about impossible to do since I'm pretty sure my face is still the shade of a fire hydrant. "Maybe I'll see you there then. We can play that game together where you throw darts at balloons, trying to pop them. If they have it, that is."

"Yeah, sure," he says.

Maybe the carnival won't be so bad after all if I can hang out with Colin for a while. I clear my throat. "Okay, let's sketch this scatter plot."

Chapter Twenty-Three
CARNIVAL PRE-PARTY

I glance at my phone as Mom maneuvers our car through Centerview, headed for Elle's house. I was texting with Nora, Anusha, and Julie just before we left. They were invited to *another* party this weekend. It's funny how their social lives went from almost nonexistent to full steam ahead at the same time mine did. Some girl named Alana, their new friend Audrey's best friend and well, I guess also their friend now, is hosting this week's drama club party at her house. I wonder if my friends are going to eventually join the drama club since they're hanging out so much with those students now? I'll be happy for them if they do. Maybe Mom will even take me home some time to watch them perform.

I've been thinking a lot about my old friends and my new friends the past couple days, and I'm starting to think this whole popularity thing isn't as great as I thought it would be. In the bigger, popular group, it feels like everyone positions themselves and uses each other to move up a peg in the group. Like it's a numbers game versus really caring about individuals. My old friends care about me and want to hear about my feelings. I don't feel like Elle truly cares about my feelings. Elle just uses me to get what she wants. But I guess I'm also guilty of that same thing since I sought her out in the first place to get in with the popular girls. Still, my old friends don't want anything from me. Even when they knew I was moving away, they still took the time to help me with Project Make Taylor Popular. I miss having close friends to talk to who really understand me.

"Are you excited to see Elle's house?" Mom asks me.

I see her looking at me in the rearview mirror and I slip my phone back into my pocket. "Yeah, sure." I briefly wonder what her house is going to look like. Elle is always dressed so well at school in trendy outfits from pricey stores. She told me once before that one of her dads orders everything for her online since the closest mall is a good forty-five minutes away. I've always appreciated how cute and coordinated she looks. My guess is that her house is going to look like one of those houses splashed across the pages of an interior design magazine. The kind of house where there aren't random papers and dishes messing up the counter but instead a mug perched purposefully on an end table to match the artwork and drapes.

"I met her dad yesterday at school when I stopped in to drop off some paperwork at the office," Mom says. "He was there to volunteer. He said he goes in once a week to help out in the library re-shelving books, covering new ones, stuff like that. Maybe I should volunteer at the school too?"

"Oh, um, if you want to," I say.

"Anyway," Mom continues, "he was so nice and friendly. He was saying that Elle just adores you and considers you one of her best friends. That's really great, Tay. I'm so happy you've made so many nice friends so quickly since we moved to Centerview. It's really put me and your dad's minds to ease that you and Sophie are doing so well here."

"Yeah, it's been really great," I tell her. My mind is still stuck on the part Mom said where Elle thinks I'm one of her best friends. Did she really tell one of her dads that? Does she actually feel that way? It makes me feel sort of guilty that I wasn't more excited to come to her pre-carnival party if she really thinks I'm one of her best friends. Not even an hour ago I was even kind of dreading it and reminding myself that at least Mackenzie would be there too.

Mom pulls the car up the driveway to Elle's house. It's a large light yellow two-story with a huge wrap-around porch. And there *is* a carefully placed mug on a small wicker table next to the porch swing. I bet it's empty and for decoration only.

I let myself out of the car after Mom puts it in park. "Want me to walk you up?" she asks.

"No, I'm fine."

"Okay, text me when you're about ready to go, and I'll pick you up in front of the school."

"Okay, bye, Mom," I say and slam the car door shut. I bounce up the steps to Elle's house and ring the doorbell. After about twenty seconds, Elle, Shriya, and Vanessa pour out of the door as they open it. I wave once more to my Mom and head inside with the girls.

We're sitting in Elle's room on the top floor of the house. It's massive, like, someone took two rooms and removed a wall or something. She has a large canopy bed in one corner that reminds me of something a princess might sleep on. A shimmery fabric has been draped along one of the walls behind the bed and lighted pink rose garland hangs all along the edges of the walls, near the ceiling. I've never seen anything like it but it's really pretty. She's got a stocked book case, a desk with a Chromebook open on it, and a couple of dressers along with an antique-looking vanity set. The vanity has a large oval mirror and a tray sitting on it piled high with makeup. There aren't any real toys anywhere in Elle's room, but she does have an enormous pink Victorian dollhouse that comes up to at least my shoulders. Part of me wants to check it out closer but I'm sure none of the other girls would want to do that. It's gorgeous and intricate filled with tiny furniture and décor. It had to cost a fortune.

Elle sits down at her vanity and studies herself in

the mirror. "We were just trying to decide how to do my hair before you got here," she explains to me. She picks up a brush and begins slowly pulling it through her hair.

Vanessa and Shriya stand up from the floor where they'd been sitting with me and stand behind Elle to also look at her reflection.

I don't really want to get up but figure I'd better join them as well.

"I think she should put it up," Vanessa says. She pulls Elle's long brown hair into a sloppy bun on top of her head.

"And I think she should wear it down," Shriya says. She moves Vanessa's hand from Elle's hair and then gives her hair a little shake, pulling pieces of it to the front near her face.

I think back to when I was still at home and Julie suggested I wear my hair in a partial bun. That would look really pretty on Elle too. "Try a partial," I say. I pull a squared portion of Elle's bangs back from her forehead and quickly twist it into a bun on top of her head. "Here, hand me a few bobby pins."

Elle reaches for a small bowl of pins and hands me some.

I expertly secure her hair and step back to survey my work. "There," I say when I'm satisfied. She looks really pretty.

Elle smiles at her reflection. "I like it. Thanks, Taylor."

"Sure." I smile back at her in the mirror and then wonder if we're each going to work on our own hairstyles now. I'd already put mine in a French braid this morning, and I'm happy with it. I don't really feel like switching styles now.

"Now let's work on Elle's makeup," Shriya says, unknowingly answering my question.

"Let me," Vanessa says, moving in front of Elle. "I was just watching a great makeup tutorial on YouTube last night for a copper glitter smoky eye. It'll really make your green eyes stand out."

Vanessa picks a few pieces of makeup off of Elle's vanity and sets to work.

I briefly wonder why we're all hovering around Elle like she's Cinderella getting ready for the ball, but I don't have to wonder for long.

"Elle has to look *amazing*," Shriya tells me. "Jackson Stone told her he'd 'see her there.' They practically have a date."

There's that word again. *Date.* I'm starting to think these girls think everything is a date.

"Hey," Lola says as she comes charging into Elle's room, Gianna and Mackenzie just steps behind. "You started without us."

"Your dad let us in," Mackenzie adds as she shrugs off her coat and tosses it onto Elle's bed.

"Ooh, I love your top, Elle," Gianna says. "Its even cuter than you described."

"Thanks," she says. She brushes an invisible piece of lint off of her shirt. As Vanessa works on Elle's makeup, Elle chatters on. "I don't know why I'm feeling nervous. I'm generally never nervous around guys."

"It's because you really like him," Lola says.

"And he's older," Mackenzie adds. "That would make me nervous."

"What are you guys going to talk about?" Gianna asks.

Elle bites her bottom lip and looks at Gianna. "I'm not sure. It'll probably come to me when I see him."

"Are we walking around with Jackson and his friends too, then?" I ask. I'm trying to envision how all of this plays out since Elle also told Daniel and them we'd be hanging out with their group.

Elle shakes her head. "No, Jackson will be running one of the booths. So, we'll have to find him and hang out by him there."

I hope she doesn't mean the whole time. I was looking forward to playing some of the games. And hopefully finding Colin too.

"Grace had better not be hanging out by him," Shriya says, her voice heavy with attitude.

I catch Mackenzie ever so slightly roll her eyes.

"Who's Grace?" I ask, obviously missing a piece of vital information.

Elle keeps her eyes closed as Vanessa expertly lines her upper lids but I can see her face tighten.

"Some ugly girl who likes Jackson, too," Shriya explains. "She's always hanging around the wrestlers."

"Elle is much prettier," Lola adds.

The girls chatter on about all of the ways that Elle is far superior to this poor girl Grace, whoever she is, and I think about how it was only a couple of months ago that I would have done anything to be sitting in the house of the most popular girl of our entire grade, giggling and having fun with a giant group of friends. I thought this was the dream. But maintaining this new life and these new relationships is seriously starting to grate on me.

I must have zoned out for a while because the next thing I know, all of the girls are on their feet and cooing about how amazing Elle looks. And she does look really nice. I'm sure Jackson will appreciate all of her efforts.

"All right, girls," Elle says, "winter carnival, here we come!"

I fall in line behind the others as we leave Elle's house and head for school.

Chapter Twenty-Four
RELATIONSHIP SHIFTS

We walk into the crowded school gym and my senses are immediately overloaded. I spot giant blue and white snowflakes covering the walls and big blue and white booths full of every carnival game imaginable. There's a loud buzz from the happily chatting students and families participating in the various activities. And right away my nostrils are filled with the scent of popcorn, hot chocolate, and cotton candy. It all seems amazing.

"Come on," Elle shouts over her shoulder and all of the girls grab hands.

We weave in and out like a snake through the lines of people waiting for various games and I try to take it all in. There's a gingerbread house mini-put put, a ball toss into buckets decorated like Santa bellies and set in a row increasing in difficulty, a knock down game of wintery decorated coffee canisters stacked in a pyramid, a holiday lollipop tree, a snow-ball throw game where you have to knock down an inflated snowman, and a balloon dart game where the balloons look like ornaments on a Christmas tree. At one station, people are doing relay races with small balloons and panty hose, trying to make rein-deer antlers to wear on their heads.

Elle pulls us to a photo booth in the corner of the gym and waves to the eighth-grade girl running it. They must be friends because the girl lets us sneak to the front of the line. I can feel the people waiting in line watching us but I try to ignore it. They might think it's unfair that we cut ahead like this but no one says anything about it. We all cram into the booth and put the funny props on: silly glasses, colorful boas, and goofy hats, and we take four pictures, altering our poses each time. The eighth grader prints out a bunch of copies of the photo strips and hands us each one.

I look down at mine and smile at it. We look so cute

and happy, like we really are the best of friends. I slip the pictures into my back pocket.

"Where to next?" Gianna asks, her face flipping back and forth between us like a windshield wiper.

"I need a drink," Lola says.

"And I'm dying for popcorn," Vanessa adds.

Elle looks around, a concerned look on her face. "Okay," she says, "but let's be quick. I want to find Jackson."

We agree to buy our food and then take a lap around the carnival to look for Jackson right after.

We wait in line at the concession stand, and I find myself searching the carnival for someone too. Colin. I wonder if he's here in this crowd somewhere with his friends or if he changed his mind and just stayed home. I wouldn't blame him if he had decided this wasn't his kind of scene.

I spot Colin standing with Steven and Owen in line for the hoop toss game. They're smiling and chatting and appear to be having a good time.

I watch Colin as he accepts three ring hoops from the eighth-grade boy running the game. He leans forward and tosses the first ring toward the rows of bottles wrapped in reindeer cozies.

I sure hope he makes it.

The first ring looked like it fell right to the ground. The hoop toss is one of the harder games. I've never been able to hoop a bottle myself when I've played. Colin tosses another ring at the bottles and misses again. He turns to say something to one of his friends, but his eyes catch mine.

Ack, there it is again! That weird feeling. There is a zing in the pit of my stomach and the hair on my arms stand up. I lift one hand and wave at him.

Colin gives me a slight nod, and I swear this time I see his cheeks pinken before he turns back to face the game. I'm feeling all warm and fluttery again.

Elle sidles up next to me and follows my gaze to Colin. She whips her head back toward me and says in a scolding whisper, "Ew, Taylor."

I frown at Elle. I'm seriously getting tired of her judge-y comments about Colin.

Elle ignores my frown and starts to walk. "Come on, guys, let's go."

I realize that I didn't even get a chance to buy my soda, but I wasn't all that thirsty anyway.

I look one more time at Colin as he takes his third toss. He misses again but I'm pretty sure he's smiling.

I hang back a few steps behind the others and walk with Mackenzie. "What's Elle's problem with Colin Wright?" I ask her. "She's so awful to him."

Mackenzie rolls her eyes and then leans toward me, blocking her lips with her fingers so the others can't see. "Rumor has it," she says in a low voice, "that Elle liked Colin in the beginning of fifth grade. She sent him one of those, check the box yes or no if you like me notes, and he checked no."

My eyebrows shoot up in surprise at this little nugget of information. "So, she's had it out for him ever since?"

"She sure can hold a grudge," Mackenzie replies.

We follow Elle and the others straight to the face-painting booth where we find Daniel, Braydon, Coleson, and Jacob standing around. Daniel is standing really close to one of the eighth-grade girls doing the face-painting. He has his face only inches away from hers, and he's laughing at something she's saying.

"Hi, guys," Elle calls out loudly when we reach them.

Daniel's eyes widen when he sees me, like he'd just been caught stealing cookies after his mom had said no more. He straightens right up.

"Hey," Jacob says.

"Hi," Coleson says.

Braydon looks down at his feet.

"H-hi there," Daniel stammers. He shifts his weight from one foot to the other.

The face-painting girl looks quizzically from Daniel to Elle and back to Daniel again.

"Whatcha guys doing?" Elle asks, narrowing her eyes at Daniel. She looks mad.

"Just uh, trying to decide what we want to have painted on our faces," Daniel replies.

Coleson and Braydon exchange a look like face paint is the last thing they'd ever have put on their faces.

I have to bite my cheeks to keep from laughing. It's so obvious what's going on here. Daniel is into the face-painting girl. Which is more than fine by me.

"Well," Elle says tersely, "you boys have fun with that. We're on a little mission ourselves so we'll be off now. Come on, girls." Elle waves her hand in the air and everyone lines up to follow her. I do, too, but not before I give Daniel a big smile and a thumb up.

He smiles back at me, looking relieved that I'm okay with everything.

When we're halfway across the gym, Elle stops in front of the ice-fishing game and turns to me. "Oh, Taylor, I'm so sorry."

The other girls circle around me.

"He's such a scum," Shriya snipes.

"He doesn't deserve you," Vanessa adds.

Lola crosses her arms and glares in Daniel's direction. "He should get a giant butt painted on his forehead."

I laugh at the image. "Guys, it's okay, really. My feelings are not hurt at all. I hope he's happy with the face-painting girl. Truly," I add.

Mackenzie puts a comforting arm around my shoulder, which is nice but not really needed because I'm seriously so fine with this new Daniel development. It actually saves me from having to let him down at some point in the future.

Elle looks at me, her eyes full of concern. "Are you really sure you're okay?"

"I'm *really* sure," I reply.

She smiles. "Okay, then if you guys don't mind, I've spotted Jackson."

"Lead the way," I tell her.

Chapter Twenty-Five
True Friends

I inwardly sigh and stretch my arms behind my back. We've been standing in the cake walk room for over half an hour now. The cake walk is in the music room across the hall from the gymnasium and away from all of the real carnival action. Jackson is in charge of the cake walk game. Mackenzie, Gianna, Lola, Vanessa, Shriya, and I have all been standing here just watching Elle flirt with Jackson and it is so, so boring. I haven't even been able to play a single game since we've gotten here.

Kids file into the room, twenty at a time, and start out by standing in a big circle. Each spot has a number on it, from one to twenty. Jackson plays music as the kids walk around and around in a circle, stepping on each number. Then when he stops the music, he picks a number out of a bowl and that kid is the winner. Only, he's been letting Elle pick the winners each time, which she finds to be a huge honor and now feels she's some kind of integral part of the game so we can't leave. Whoever Elle picks gets to go pick out a cake from the long rows of tables stocked deep with cakes donated by the mothers. And then those twenty kids leave and another twenty kids file in. This continues until either all of the cakes have been given away or we lapse into a coma from sheer boredom.

I stifle a yawn and crack my neck as the next round of twenty kids file in. I would seriously rather be taking a district standardized test right now. Or even a visit to the dentist. At least then I'd get a small prize on the way out. I look over the new group of cake-walkers as they fill out the circle and suddenly I perk right up. Colin is here! He and his friends wandered in at the tail end of this group. I smile at him and wave.

He waves back and sort of sheepishly shrugs as he takes a place on the closest number.

Jackson starts up the music and the kids walk around and around the circle. Colin, Steve, and Owen are sort of goofing around as they walk to the music, smacking at each other and being silly. I hope one of them wins the cake this time.

"Yikes," Elle says loudly as the guys pass by us, "who let the losers in?"

Jackson gives Elle an alarmed look but Shriya and Vanessa laugh like it's the funniest thing they've ever heard in their entire lives.

"Hey," Elle says even louder now, "it really is a carnival. We have our own real life freakshow!"

"Elle, stop it!" I snap, worried that Colin and his friends might hear her nasty words. I shoot daggers at her with my eyes.

Jackson looks down at Elle, a slight look of disgust on his face. If Elle was doing this to impress Jackson, then she's sorely misjudged her audience, because I don't think he's finding her nearly so charming anymore.

Colin rounds the corner again and suddenly it is as if everything is moving in slow motion. Elle sticks out one booted foot right in front of Colin, tripping him, and sending him flying face first into a full sheet chocolate cake with big, puffy, red, blue, and yellow icing balloons sitting atop thick white frosting.

Jackson slams off the music and the entire room erupts into laughter. Elle, Shriya, and Vanessa are laughing so hard that there are tears rolling down their cheeks. Lola, Gianna, and Mackenzie are looking on in shock.

I am horrified.

Colin just lays there, face down in the cake for a few moments, shocked as well, I'm sure.

"Whoops, sorry," Elle says sarcastically, still snickering.

Colin slowly pushes himself up out of the cake, stands, and turns around, his face and the front of his hair covered in frosting. He puts up both of his hands and wipes at his eyes so he can see. He looks at Elle and our friends, and then at me, his eyes lingering a beat longer on mine. He turns and heads for the door. His friends are close behind him.

My heart is completely wrenching at the humiliation he must be feeling. "Colin, wait!" I call out and start to go after him.

Elle tugs at my arm. "Let him go, Taylor, he's such a loser."

To say that I am beyond furious with her would be an understatement. I'm so mad, I can feel myself shaking. I ball my hands into fists at my sides and turn to face Elle, aware that the entire room is now watching us. "No, he's not!" I yell loudly at her. The room is dead silent, and my friends are all watching me with huge eyes. I take a deep breath because I have more to say to her, and I want her to hear me clearly. "You know who's a loser, *Elle*?" I say, emphasizing her name. "People like *you* who need to knock others down to build themselves up."

Elle gasps and takes a step back from me, like I'd struck her.

"It's not cool," I continue, "the way you treat people you don't deem special enough to be in your little group, and I'm done standing by and watching you stomp on everyone else around you."

Elle's cheeks go pink and she looks around nervously from our friends to the crowd of cake walk participants watching our confrontation with rapt attention. "Whatever, Taylor," she says in a shaky voice, stumbling for words, "I always knew you were a total loser, too."

A slow grin begins to spread across my face. "That's actually not true," I say, matter-of-factly. "You had no idea."

I start to turn to leave and then stop. "You know," I say looking back at her, "I actually feel sorry for you, Elle. Eventually you're going to run out of people to put down, and then you'll just have to deal with yourself." I put both of my hands in the air in a final wave. "I'm outta here."

With that, I turn around and head for the door. I don't look back, but I do hear Jackson say to Elle, "You can go too. I don't need any more of your help." I smile to myself. I like this Jackson kid.

I walk quickly down the hallway, trying to figure out where Colin ran off to and I hear Mackenzie calling out my name.

"Taylor! Taylor, wait up!"

I stop walking and turn around, happy to see my friend.

Mackenzie rushes up to me and throws her arms around my neck, squeezing tight. When she pulls back, she looks me in the eyes and says, "That. Was. Awesome."

I giggle and put my hands over my lips, as it hits me what just happened.

"You just did," Mackenzie continues, "what probably

every kid in our grade has wanted to do since forever. You're a hero."

I wave a hand at her like it wasn't that big of a deal even though I know it was.

"Are you looking for Colin?" she asks me.

"Yeah," I reply. "I want to make sure he's okay."

Mackenzie nods in a direction over my right shoulder. "There he is now."

I turn around and see Colin coming out of the boys' bathroom. He stops in place when he sees me. The front of his hair is wet from cleaning the cake off of his face. I know he's upset, but I can't help thinking he looks really, really cute with his hair all wet and messy like this.

I rush up to him, and Mackenzie is right behind me. I grab both of his arms with my hands. "Are you okay? Elle is horrible. That was so completely wrong what she did to you."

Colin shrugs and casts his eyes downward. "I'm fine," he says.

I can tell he's embarrassed, and it hurts my heart that he's hurting.

"I'm so, so sorry that happened," I say.

"It's fine, really," he insists, still unable to meet my eyes.

"Colin, you should have seen Taylor go off on Elle just now for doing that to you," Mackenzie says excitedly. "She totally humiliated her in front of all those people. It was so completely epic."

Colin lifts his head, and his eyes meet mine. His mouth falls open in shock and he looks back and forth between me and Mackenzie. "Really?" he asks me.

I bite my bottom lip and nod.

"But, she's your friend," he says.

I shake my head. "Not anymore."

We lock eyes, and he beams at me.

I feel that tingly feeling in my stomach again, just like the last couple of times Colin has looked at me like that.

Mackenzie clears her throat, reminding us that she's standing there.

"Where are your friends?" I ask, suddenly noticing that they're not around.

"I told them I'd meet them back inside the gym after I cleaned up," he says.

I look at Mackenzie and then back at Colin. "Do you mind if we hang out with you guys?"

"Of course not," he says happily and the three of us head back into the gym together.

We spot Steven and Owen right away, chatting and munching on popcorn. They come straight over and join our group.

"Everything cool now?" Owen asks.

I look at Colin to see his reply.

"We're all good," he says.

And he's right. We *are* all good. I look from Mackenzie to Colin to Colin's friends, who will hopefully end up being mine someday, too. And I think about my friends back home, Anusha, Nora, and Julie. I realize that I never really needed to surround myself with a giant group of friends to be happy. I just need a few who really matter.

"Where to first?" Colin asks me.

I look around the gym, at all the kids and families talking and laughing, playing games, and eating hot dogs and pizza, and my eyes zero in on the giant cotton candy machine in the corner. I grin at my friends. "How about some cotton candy? On me."

"My favorite," Colin says and the others nod.

We make our way through the crowded gym, Colin and I behind the others, and I can hear Mackenzie telling Steven and Owen a funny story about something she saw on You Tube the night before. I'm feeling truly happy in this moment and excited to finally have some fun at this school carnival with people I really like. I've grown so much since moving to Centerview. It feels like my disaster of a party and my birthday wish to be popular was a million years ago. This is what I should have wished for. This is perfect.

As we walk, I feel Colin slip his hand into mine and my heart practically stops. I actually don't think I'm breathing. I can't look at him, but I close my fingers around his. I can feel myself grinning from ear to ear. Perfect.

SWIRL

Pumpkin Spice Secrets
by Hillary Homzie

Sometimes secrets aren't so sweet . . .

When Maddie spills her pumpkin spice drink on a cute boy, she's instantly smitten. But add best friend drama and major school stress to Maddie's secret coffee shop crush, and it's a recipe for disaster. Can she stay true to both her friend and her heart?

Sky Pony Press
New York

SW🥤RL

Peppermint Cocoa Crushes
by Laney Nielson

Friends, cocoa, crushes...catastrophe!

'Tis the season for snow, gifts, peppermint cocoa, and the school's variety show competition! But Sasha's head is spinning between rehearsals, homework, and volunteer commitments. Can she make the most of her moment in the spotlight?

Sky Pony Press
New York

Cinnamon Bun Besties

by Stacia Deutsch

It's bestie vs. bestie . . .

When the Valentine's Day fundraiser Suki is running gets out of control and the local animal shelter where she volunteers is in danger of closing, she's determined to save the day. But she can't do it alone—and her only hope for help is her worst enemy . . .

Sky Pony Press
New York

SWIRL

Salted Caramel Dreams

by Jackie Nastri Bardenwerper

Friendship without drama? Dream on!

Jasmine has always been best friends with Kiara. They have a secret handshake, a plan to open a joint Etsy shop, and even invented a salted caramel drink together at the local cafe. But when Kiara joins the basketball team, she starts to become distant . . . and then she betrays Jasmine's trust.

Sky Pony Press
New York

SWIRL

Apple Pie Promises

by Hillary Homzie

A new stepsister, an old crush, and the best Fall Festival of all time. Bring on the drama!

Lily's mom has gotten a once-in-a-lifetime work opportunity in Africa and will be gone for a year, so Lily is moving in with her dad—and new stepmom and stepsister—right in time for the Fall Festival. Sharing a bedroom is one thing, but sharing a crush is another . . .

Sky Pony Press
New York